SUNSHINE AND STARFISH

(Summer at the Seaside)

Regina Walker

Check out the latest about Regina Walker at
reginawalkerauthor.com.

Sunshine and Starfish

Scripture quotations are taken from the *Holy Bible*, New Living Translation, copyright © 1996, 2004, 2015 by Tyndale House Foundation. Used by permission of Tyndale House Publishers, Inc., Carol Stream, Illinois 60188. All rights reserved.

Sunshine and Starfish is a work of fiction. Where real people, events, establishments, organizations, or locales appear, they are used fictitiously. All other elements of the novel are drawn from the author's imagination.

Cover by Virginia McKevitt.

Published in the United States of America by:
Regina Walker
PO Box 492
Jones, Oklahoma 73049

To my sister, Adriane.

You give 110% plus some in all that you do. You make the world a better place, and I'm better for knowing you. Thank you for all of your love and support.

Dear brothers and sisters, when troubles of any kind come your way, consider it an opportunity for great joy. For you know that when your faith is tested, your endurance has a chance to grow. So let it grow, for when your endurance is fully developed, you will be perfect and complete, needing nothing.

JAMES 1:2-4 NLT

Contents

Chapter One   9

Chapter Two   25

Chapter Three   39

Chapter Four   47

Chapter Five   55

Chapter Six   63

Chapter Seven   73

Chapter Eight   87

Chapter Nine   95

Chapter Ten   101

Chapter Eleven   109

Chapter Twelve   113

Chapter Thirteen   123

Chapter Fourteen   131

Epilogue   137

Summer at the Seaside   140

Also by Regina Walker   151

About the Author   156

Chapter One

Jane

Standing on the wrong side of what she assumed was a loaded gun, Jane Everly silently thanked God for giving her a good life while pulling the cash from her register and putting it in the bag.

"Hurry up, lady," the male voice demanded.

He sounded young, Jane thought, and she glanced up at him. The black mask pulled over his face concealed his identity, but she wondered whether he was a local or not.

"You can have it all. I'm getting it," she said. Her voice was gentle, and she tried to sound reassuring. Tingling started in her toes and creeped over her foot and slowly up her legs. She felt the tension of fear in every fiber of her body. She started with the ones, then the fives, then the tens. Cramming the bills in the bag, she scooted each stack of cash over to make room for the next.

She thought the bag was so small he must have known he wasn't robbing something as prolific as a bank. She wondered if he would rob another store after hers, or if he had robbed one beforehand. She took another glance at him.

The gun wobbled in his hand, and he raised the barrel higher, pointing it more at her chest than her stomach. "I said hurry up!"

"I am, I am," Jane said. Her hands trembled and she fumbled as she pulled the twenties from the drawer and crammed them in the bag. She always thought she'd cry if she found herself in this situation, but no tears came to her eyes. The tingling reached her knees and she thought they might buckle and leave her in a heap on the floor.

Her front door alert, the sound of a dog barking three times, brought her gaze straight up toward the front door.

"I'm sorry, we're closed. Come back tomorrow, please," she said to the man that walked in. Unfamiliar, he stared over at her, a white boxer with brindle spots at his side.

"I just need a bag of dog food," the man said.

The young male spun and pointed the gun at the man. "She said she's closed!" The gunman shouted at the man who stood frozen in the doorway. His gun wielding hand trembled, and the gun shook back and forth.

"Whoa, whoa, it's alright, I just needed some dog food." The man lifted his hands, one held his dog's leash, the other was empty and open.

"We're good. You can go," Jane called over.

"Under the till," the robber spun on her,

pointing the gun at her head. "Get it all!"

Jane nodded. "I'm getting it." Her shaking hands yanked the upper part of the drawer out, revealing her two one-hundred-dollar bills and a fifty. She put them in his bag and then pushed the bag toward him. "It's all in there."

"Do you have a safe?" He waved the gun, still aimed at her head.

"No, no safe. This is just a small pet store and it's been slow today," Jane said.

The boxer started growling and the man tugged his leash. "Easy boy."

"I'll shoot him if he comes after me," the masked man shouted. He spun, pointing the gun at the man and dog again. "Where's the back door?" he asked Jane.

She pointed at the closed door behind her. "Straight through there. The deadbolt is locked. It'll let you out in the alley." She held her hands up so he could see them.

"Nobody moves for three minutes," he ordered. He bolted through the door behind her, jogged to the exit door, and disappeared into the alley.

Jane looked over at the man and raised a brow. "Are you okay?"

"Am I okay?" His tone was a mix of shock and sympathy. He strode to the counter. "Are *you* okay?"

Jane nodded stoically and reassembled her cash register. "Your dog food is on me today. Just grab what you need and let me scan it so I can count it in my inventory, please."

She turned her back to him and grabbed the cordless phone off its wall-mounted base. Punching in 9-1-1, she held the phone to her head and listened to it ring.

"Yes, this is Jane at the Granby Pet Store. I was just held up... I'm fine... No injuries... Yes, one customer came in during the robbery... He's fine... No, the man is gone... Yes, okay... I'll be here, thank you."

When she turned, she jerked from surprise because the man was still standing at her counter.

"Are you sure you're okay?" he asked.

"I'm fine. Really. I think he was just a kid," Jane said.

The boxer at the man's side jumped up, placing his paws on the counter. One ear sported the brindle coloring, while his other ear and the rest of his head was white. Jane reached both hands forward and stroked the sides of his face and rubbed his ears.

"What's his name?" she asked.

"This is L.T., he's my road dog," he said.

"Road dog?" Jane asked.

"Yep, he rides in my truck with me. Do you want me to stay until the police arrive?" he asked.

"Oh no, really. It's fine. You can just grab your dog food and go," she said.

He looked over his shoulder toward the front door, and then leaned to his right, looking through the door to the back. The door to the alley was open and sunlight streamed in.

"Want me to close that door?" He pointed.

Jane let her eyelids fall over her eyes for a long blink and she swallowed, fighting back the snappy tone that she felt coming. "Sir, I appreciate your kindness, but I'm fine. I'd like to just sweep up this mess back here," she gestured toward the shattered remains of a ceramic pet bowl on the floor at her feet, "and get back to my day."

She studied his expression and saw a firm, but quiet, resolve etched in the lines around his baby blue eyes. His short-cut strawberry blond hair matched his eyebrows and short beard. Their eyes met and he smiled at her, something peaceful and reassuring about his expression caused her shoulders to relax a little bit.

The tingling started to drain down her legs and normal feeling returned. As her heart rate slowed, exhaustion settled deep into her bones.

Thank you, God. Thank you for sparing my life and this man's life. Please stop that kid and help him find a better way.

Her eyes closed for another long blink and when she opened them, the man had moved away from the counter toward the first aisle of dog food.

"I have a lot of those in bigger bags, if you want more than five or fifteen pounds," Jane said.

"Thank you," he said, peering over a shelf at her. "I'm Hayden, by the way."

"Hayden?" she questioned.

13

"Yes?" he asked, his expression serious.

She laughed a little bit and shook her head. "Just making sure I heard you right, is all."

A modest grin tugged his lips upward and he chuckled. "I know. Did that with a straight face, too."

Her hand went to her mouth, and she laughed, shaking her head slightly. "Are you always this ornery?"

"Usually," he confessed.

The barking dog door chime turned her attention toward the front door, while making L.T. bark twice in his loud, deep voice.

"We got a report of a robbery here?" Two female officers walked through the front door.

"I'm Officer Jackson," the female officer with light brown skin stepped up to the counter. Arranged in neat braids, her dark hair hung half an inch above the collar of her shirt. She gestured toward her partner. "This is Officer Martin. Is everyone okay?"

"We're fine. I'm fine," Jane laid her hand on her chest to indicate herself. "Are you sure you're okay, Hayden?"

"Right as rain," he said. He walked out where the officers could see him and his dog.

"Did you know your door in the back is open?" Officer Martin asked, gesturing toward the door in the back that let out into the alley.

"That's the way the man... boy, rather, ran out," Jane said.

"How old do you think the suspect was?" Officer Jackson asked.

"Oh, I'm not sure. Maybe sixteen or seventeen," Jane answered.

"Can you describe him for me?" Officer Jackson asked. She held a small notebook and pen in her hand, taking notes.

"Do you mind?" Officer Martin tipped her head toward the back room.

"Go ahead," Jane said.

With her hand on her gun, Officer Martin disappeared into the back room, toward the open door.

"He was sixteen or seventeen. Scared. Had a gun. He kept shaking. He was pointing it low but the more agitated he got, he would raise it. Before he left, he was pointing it right at my head," Jane said. She rubbed her hand across her forehead. Fatigue set deep into her muscles and bones. She was ready for bed, and it wasn't even three in the afternoon yet.

"How tall was he?"

"My height. I'm five foot five. He wasn't taller than me. He kept telling me to hurry. He brought a bag with him. Just a small, black bag. I was thinking he couldn't rob more than one place at a time without emptying the bag. He knew he wasn't getting thousands of dollars here." Jane leaned against the counter.

Hayden watched her intently, reaching forward, he patted the back of her hand. "You did a good job staying calm when he was here."

"What was he wearing?" Officer Jackson asked.

"A black mask," Jane said.

"Did you see his other clothes?" Officer Jackson asked.

Jane thought for a minute and scrunched up her shoulders, holding them for a long beat, then lowering them. "I wasn't paying attention to his clothes. I just wanted him to stay calm and not shoot."

"Do you know what kind of gun he had?" Officer Jackson asked.

Jane laughed at that and pressed her hand against the counter to steady herself. "No idea. I don't know anything about guns. It was black."

"It was a Stoeger forty," Hayden said.

"Did you get a good look at the guy?" Officer Jackson asked.

"She's right, he was probably five-five. A hundred and fifteen pounds, if. White male, scared. Thin. He was wearing an orange t-shirt and blue jeans. His shoes were worn out. Gray. Generic. But I could see his socks on his toes on one foot. He was probably sixteen or seventeen, like she said." Hayden lifted his hand toward Jane.

"And your name is?" Officer Jackson asked.

"Hayden Moore, Ma'am."

"Are you from around here?" the officer asked.

"No, ma'am. I'm just in town overnight. Taking my ten-hour break, then I'll be on my way. I drive a truck," he said.

Officer Martin, fair skinned, freckled, and sporting fire red hair in a tight bun, appeared at the front door and strode over to her partner.

"Anything?" Officer Jackson asked.

"Back is clear. Do you have a description? I can ask around, see if anyone saw him before or after he came in here," Officer Martin said.

The officers stepped off to the side to talk for a moment, so Officer Jackson could relay the suspect description.

"Did you find your dog food?" Jane asked Hayden.

"Oh, yeah. You've got it. The Earthborn Holistic in the blue bag. I'll grab it in a minute. I need some flea and tick stuff and I thought I might use your self-wash bay and give L.T. here a bath. He hasn't had one in a couple of weeks. I was looking for a shampoo for white coats when they got here," he said, his head tipping slightly toward the officers.

"I don't have any whitening shampoo, but I do have a probiotic shampoo in the wash bay. You are welcome to use that," Jane said.

Officer Jackson stepped back to the counter, looking at her notes. "I just have a few more questions for you, Jane."

"Absolutely, anything," Jane said.

"Did this kid seem familiar to you?" Officer Jackson asked.

Hayden gestured toward the wash bay and pointed at L.T., trying not to interrupt as he excused himself to go wash his dog.

"How much do you think he got away with?" Officer Jackson looked up from her notes, her eyebrow raised at Jane.

"Oh gosh, let me think here, there were two one-hundred-dollar bills and a fifty, but the twenties...hmmm," she tapped her fingers on the counter and then her eyes widened with recognition, "I can just run my report. I started my till with three hundred dollars this morning." Jane turned to her sales screen and tapped a few buttons. "Looks like I had three twenty-seven in sales. So, he made off with six twenty-seven."

"Do you have any security cameras inside or out?" Officer Jackson asked.

"No. I've never had anything like this happen before. Do you think it will happen again?" Jane asked.

"Hard to tell. Sometimes thieves will hit the same place a couple of times if it was easy enough and they got enough money. Some thieves never hit the same place twice. I think I have everything I need for my report." Officer Jackson reached into her pocket and pulled a business card out. "Here's my card, call me if you think of anything or need anything."

"Wait, aren't you going to dust for fingerprints or something?" Jane asked.

The chuckle from Hayden as he brought a cleaned and dried L.T. out of the self-wash center turned both Officer Jackson and Jane's heads. Jane looked confused, but Officer Jackson's expression was cross. She turned back to Jane.

"We don't dust for prints. There are probably thousands of prints in this place, and we can't put in the hours to identify all of those people as proper customers versus the robber. I'm sorry," Officer Jackson said.

"So, what are you going to do?" Jane asked.

"Ask a few other businesses if they have cameras, if they saw anything in the alley, cross check with any calls of suspicious activity. That's about all we can do," Officer Jackson said.

"Am I safe?" Jane asked, her voice softer.

"I think you probably are. Sounds like a teen that got in a jam. Not that it's okay and I know you probably feel violated, but I don't think you're in any imminent danger," Officer Jackson said.

Hayden walked closer to the counter, waving as Officer Jackson excused herself.

"That's it?" Jane turned to him, her eyebrows lifted, her expression somber.

"There isn't much else they can do. You should put up some security cameras," Hayden said.

"I don't know how to do that," Jane said.

"Do you have someone that could help you do it?" Hayden asked.

Jane's mind drifted twenty years back, to the night of her third wedding anniversary. A night that most couples would have been celebrating with a fancy dinner, or a weekend getaway, she was crouched at the edge of a hospital bed,

19

listening to the final breaths of her dying husband. She'd been alone ever since.

Cliff would have put up cameras for her, if he'd lived long enough. Looking at the stranger across the counter from her, she offered a faint smile in his direction, then she grabbed a tub of wipes and started cleaning off the counter.

"I could ask someone from church," she said.

"Church?" He cocked a brow and scoffed. "No husband or brother you could ask?"

She thought of her brother-in-law, but it was a three-hour drive for him and her sister to reach Granby, North Carolina. They were both busy with an upcoming college graduation and a high school graduation for their two kids.

"I'm sure someone at church would be happy to help. Hopefully they can tell me where to buy security cameras," she said.

"Amazon. Sam's Club. Best Buy. There are plenty of places that sell them," Hayden leaned his hip against the counter. "How much do I owe you for the dog wash and a bag of dog food?"

"It's on me today. Sorry you've spent all afternoon tied up here. You didn't have to—"

Hayden waved a hand in the air. "Stop that. Don't tell me I didn't have to. You were on the wrong end of a loaded firearm; I'm impressed that you're still standing and haven't closed up shop and gone home for the day."

"I can't do that; my customers are counting on me to be consistent. Consistency is important, you know."

"Yeah, yeah it is." Hayden nodded slowly. He tugged his wallet free from his back pocket and opened it. Pulling a hundred-dollar bill out, he set it on the counter, then turned, grabbed his dog food, and headed for the exit.

"Wait," Jane called, "that's too much. You can't just leave that lying there."

He didn't turn or answer her.

"Hayden," she said as he pushed the door open and let the salty sea breeze enter the store, but he still didn't respond.

Hayden

"Granby, Mom, Granby, North Carolina," Hayden said into the phone.

L.T. sat in the passenger seat, watching everything out of the windshield as they cruised down the interstate at a steady seventy miles per hour.

"G-R-A-N-B as in boy-Y. Granby. Yes," he said.

"I still don't understand why I'm sending security cameras to an address in Granby, North Carolina. Who do you know there?" his mom asked.

"I just met her. In the middle of a robbery. She

21

needs security cameras for her store," he said.

"But why doesn't she buy them herself?" his mom fired back.

"Because, she doesn't have anyone to put them up. I mean, she said someone from church would do it, but honestly, Mom, when is the last time someone from church did something like that?" Hayden asked.

"Oh boy, I know that's right. Did she really say that?" His mom kind of chuckled, which made her cough.

Hayden listened as she lost her breath from the onslaught of hacking coughs. Once they got started there was nothing he could do but wait and think over and over in his mind, *breathe Momma, breathe. Easy. I wish this would go away.*

"I thought I might go install them for her when I'm back down there next week. That's why I need you to order the cameras now, so they have a chance to get there," Hayden said.

"Are you coming home right now?" she asked, her voice tired and raspy.

"Yes, Momma. I'm coming home. I've got almost thirteen hundred miles to run, so I won't be home until tomorrow, but this time it's my thirty-four-hour break. You rest now. We can order the cameras later," he said.

"Son, I've already got your cameras ordered. Says she'll have them one week from today," his mom said, still sounding spent.

"Do you need to rest now?" he asked.

He heard the fight start in her voice. It wasn't long ago she would have told him to mind his own business, that she would tell him when she needed to rest but he wouldn't tell her when to rest. Lung cancer was taking a toll on her, though. She didn't argue as much, and she gave in more easily when he suggested she rest or nap. He knew he would only be home long enough to take her to her chemo appointment on Monday, and then he'd have to take her home and leave her. He thought about the nurse he'd hired and how grateful he was for her dedicated care, but even she wasn't available twenty-four hours a day.

He couldn't begrudge the woman of her husband and children. She needed a life outside of caring for his mother, but what he wanted was for her to be there every second he couldn't.

"Hayden," her voice was weak, "I'm going to rest. I have to," she said.

"I know. I love you," he said.

"I love you forever, son," she replied.

He waited for her to hang up. When the line went dead, his grip on the steering wheel tightened. He hoped he was wrong, but it seemed like her new treatment was failing just like her last treatment. Her doctor said they only had one more thing to try after this and then it would be time for hospice. Hospice at sixty-five? Shouldn't that be when his mom was retired and able to start living her life?

The miles ticked by, one at a time, slow and

steady. He reached over and rubbed the top of L.T.'s head. "All you did was growl at that guy. I always thought I'd be hard pressed to hold your leash if something bad was happening, but you didn't seem inclined to go after him. You just ride along for the snacks, don't you?" Hayden fished a piece of beef jerky out of the open bag in his cup holder.

"Want this?" He wiggled it toward L.T. who whimpered and started wiggling in his seat. Hayden fed him the beef jerky and grinned, scratching behind his dog's ears.

"Just the treats. You're no bodyguard. I sure thought better of you than that. Silly dog." Hayden turned up the radio and hammered down. "Oklahoma, here we come."

Chapter Two

Jane

"Hey Bobby," Jane smiled at her regular UPS driver. He carried a box to the counter, holding his handheld up.

"Need a signature on this one, Jane," he said.

She signed the device and shook her head. "Never looks right on there. I swear I write better than that."

"Oh, I know. I hear that all the time," Bobby said. "How've you been since the robbery? Are you feeling okay being here alone all day?"

Jane gritted her teeth and nodded. "I'm fine. I try not to think about it, honestly."

Bobby tilted his head to the side. "What else can you do, right?"

"Hire security," she said, laughing.

"You really could. There are firms in the city that specialize in small business security," Bobby said, his expression growing serious.

"No, Bobby. I'm a small pet shop. I just hope the kid doesn't come back. The detectives haven't figured out who he is yet," Jane said. "Do you need food for Poe?"

"Still have half a bag, I'll get some in a week. I've got to run; you know how this thing is. Tells me how many minutes I'm expected to be at this stop." He waved his handheld in the air and turned to leave. His boots thumped across the concrete floor.

Jane opened the package and stared at a box of six white security cameras. She slid her fingers over the shrink wrap around the box before turning to the wall-mounted base and grabbing her cordless phone. She punched in a number from memory.

"Pastor Clark, how are you today... I'm great... I thought we decided to order black cameras for the store... well the ones that were delivered are white..."

The barking dog door chime brought her attention to the front door where her postal carrier, Megan, brought in a box and a stack of letters.

Jane put her hand over the cordless phone's microphone. "I wasn't expecting another box today." She brought the phone back up to her ear. "Pastor, hey, Megan is here with another box, I've got to run. White cameras are fine, I'm not even worried about it... You too... Bye now." She returned the phone to its base and accepted the box from Megan.

"How are you holding up? I heard at Bible study last night what happened to you, and I just feel sick over it."

"I'm okay, thank you. Just trying to move forward the best that I can," Jane said.

"I know you are, hun. I'm just worried about you being here alone all day. What about getting a gun?" Megan asked.

"We didn't need two guns in that fight. I knew right then that I would never carry, just like I always said. I could never harm someone in that way, or possibly take their life."

"Even defending your own life and property?" Megan asked.

"Even then," Jane answered.

"What about saving the lives of innocent bystanders, like your customers?" Megan asked.

Jane closed her eyes and shook her head from side to side. "Not even then. I just couldn't bring myself to shoot someone."

"Well, if you need anything at all, you call me, you got it? I'll do anything I can to help you. We all agreed we would pool together and replace the money that was stolen," Megan said.

Jane waved her hands in the air, shooing Megan toward the door. "I don't need the money. Honestly. I'm just afraid he'll come back and be more brazen. I keep praying about it and I know it's going to be fine. I never really wanted cameras, but I was glad when they arrived. Now, I just need to get them installed."

"Is anyone helping you with that?" Megan hovered at the front door.

"Pastor Clark is gathering a few guys together Saturday. They all know how to do this kind of stuff. So, I'm going to close the store for the day. I've been giving everyone that comes in a flyer announcing the closure, and my sister posted it on the internet on that page she made for me."

"Facebook?" The right corner of Megan's mouth tugged upward in a lopsided grin as she shook her head.

"I think so," Jane nodded, and then waved her hands in a shooing motion, "back to work, Megs."

Jane turned to the box she'd taken from Megan, and she opened the top of it. Inside were the black cameras she thought she was opening when the white ones arrived. She tapped her finger on top of the box of cameras, then slid it out of her arms onto her counter. The three dog barks signaled her front door opening again and she looked up.

"Hey Stasia, here to give Patches a bath?"

"Sure am. Can't have her getting matted up." Trotting beside Stasia, looking fancy and like quite the lady, was a black and white Lhasa Apso. The pair disappeared into the self-wash station and Jane listened to Stasia sing to the little dog.

"Must have been quite the fright for you, hmmm?" Stasia poked her head out of the self-washroom, standing on her tippy toes to see Jane.

"It was." The admission still made Jane feel sick to her stomach. She didn't want to be afraid of a masked stranger that may never return, but the truth was, every time the front door barked at her, she felt like collapsing behind the counter.

Barking three times, the front door drew Jane out of her thoughts once again. Ainsley walked in, her long, golden blonde hair hanging over her shoulders and down her back. Her book bag was hoisted over one shoulder, and she walked behind the counter with Jane. "I already know what happened, and I know you're going to tell me I can't watch the store in the evenings for you because of it. But I won't let you tell me no. You need a break and I need a job."

"Ainsley, you don't understand. He came in with a gun, demanding all the money." Jane felt the weakness in her voice. It twisted to her core and made her want to go home and curl up in bed, under the covers.

"Fine. He had a gun, and he wanted the money. If it happens again, I'll do like you did and give him the money. I won't give him any attitude and I won't try to stop him or be the hero. So, did you count the drawer down to three hundred already, or do you want me to do that while you start the closing spreadsheet for mc?"

"I'll count down the till," Jane said.

"I sure like that shampoo you have in there. It cleared up all of Patches flaky skin." Stasia sauntered to the counter. "I'm going to need a bag of dog food and treats, too. You know what I get, I never remember."

From the supply on the shelves, Jane selected the dog food and treats that Stasia used and then rang them up, along with the self-wash. After taking the money and double checking with Ainsley, Jane walked Stasia and Patches to their car.

"I'm not much of a hugger, but you sure look like you could use one." Stasia lowered the little black and white dog into the passenger seat of the car while Jane put her dog food and treats in the backseat.

"I'm okay. It's just been a long week," Jane said.

"I'm sure it has. Are you sleeping?" Stasia asked.

Jane looked over the top of the car, across the street to the row of shops and vacant storefronts. She took a deep breath and slowly let it out. "No, Stasia. I haven't been able to sleep much."

"You might talk to your doctor. They have a lot of options, especially for short term sleep disruptions." Stasia closed the gap between her and Jane and wrapped Jane in a big hug, holding it for longer than Jane normally would have preferred, but in the midst of all the chaos, she was thankful for the embrace.

"See you at church on Sunday." Jane waved at Stasia and then returned to the pet store.

Before the front door even closed behind Jane,

Ainsley was talking to her. "I counted the till, I started the closing spreadsheet, and I rinsed the tub in the self-wash. You can go now."

"Cool your jets," Jane said.

"I just don't want you to think you can't take a break. My mom said you've worked in this store for ten hours a day, six days a week, for as long as she could remember, until you hired me. I know you trust me. I love this store. Please go relax," Ainsley said.

"Fine, fine. I'll go." Jane's steps landed heavier than she meant as she passed the girl and went into the back room. Retrieving her small, teal purse and her keys, she passed back by the counter on her way toward the front door. "Promise you'll call if you need anything? It won't be dark when you're leaving but pay attention to your surroundings."

"Got it, bye!" Ainsley leaned over the counter to wave at Jane.

Hayden

March was coming to a warm end and Saturday was particularly lovely. Hayden backed into the truck stop on the edge of Granby and spent a few minutes settling in. He ordered an Uber and then took L.T. to walk in the grass. When his Uber arrived, he double checked that his truck was locked, swung his tool bag into the backseat of the car, and got in with his dog.

"Do you know where the Granby Pet Store is?" Hayden asked the woman driving the car.

Her brown eyes were kind as she looked at him in the reviewer mirror. "I do, is that where we are headed?" She asked in her heavy Spanish accent.

"Yeah," Hayden said. "Where are you from?"

"Guatemala, but I've been here for ten years. I hope to never leave," she said. "I'm Juliana. But you can call me Julie. Where are you from?"

"Sooner born, Sooner bred, and when I die, I'll be Sooner dead."

"Sooner?" She raised an eyebrow at him, glancing back in the mirror as she navigated the quiet streets of Granby.

"I'm from Oklahoma." Hayden rubbed L.T.'s head and watched as the picturesque little town passed by his window.

"What's your dog's name?" Julie asked.

"This is L.T. I've had him for about five years. Since he was a six-week-old pup. His head was so big that his back legs would come off the ground when he was eating."

L.T. started panting louder and reached his nose over the seat toward Julie, as if he knew they were talking about him.

"He's the best dog I've ever owned," Hayden said.

"What kind is he?" Julie asked.

"He's a boxer. Do you have any pets?"

"Oh no, no. I have no pets. But someday I might have a dog," she said.

She pulled the car up in front of the pet store and Hayden got out with his tool bag and his dog. "Thanks for the ride."

"Anytime. Enjoy your stay in Granby," she said.

Hayden strolled through the propped open front door of the pet store and looked around. Three guys, all on ladders, worked on hanging black cameras in the corners and behind the counter.

"I really thought I ordered white cameras," Hayden said when Jane came out of the back.

"You ordered the white cameras?" Her long black hair was straight and shiny, and she stared at him with the most captivating blue-green eyes. He had never seen eyes so crystal clear or bright.

"I ordered the white cameras. I wanted to make sure you got them put up. Today was the soonest I could get back." *Even though I should be home with my mom.* Shame over leaving his sick mother to come help a stranger gnawed at his insides.

"Pastor Clark helped me order these black ones, and they are getting them installed now," she said.

"Any outdoor cameras or motion sensors?" Hayden asked.

Jane shook her head. "Not as far as I know."

"Well, we will create you an indoor and

outdoor system by combining both camera sets. That way everything is covered. I can get to work on installing the outside cameras."

Before Jane could protest or disagree, Hayden was grabbing a ladder from the backroom and heading outside. He propped the ladder against the brick wall and climbed up until he could reach the roof overhang on the northwest corner of her shop.

He marked the wood where the mount should be screwed in, then readied his drill. He forgot his safety glasses and grumbled a little since he'd be drilling above his head.

"Hey," a male voice called up to him.

Hayden peered down at the man dressed in black basketball shorts and a blue t-shirt. The cross on the shirt made Hayden think the guy must be from the church Jane mentioned. "Hey."

"I'm Clark. Could I get you to come down here for a minute?" Clark wore an inviting enough smile.

"Okay." Hayden put his drill back in his work belt and tucked the camera under his arm, then he shimmied down the ladder. "What can I do for you, Clark?"

"I just thought maybe our efforts would all accomplish more if we worked together. I've got six guys here installing things. We didn't know where those cameras came from," Clark pointed at the white camera in Hayden's hand, "but now that we do, if you want to use them, we can all work together."

"I'm good, I'll just put these up outside," Hayden said.

Jane leaned out of the doorway, looking right at Hayden. His eyes met hers and instead of spinning around to the ladder, he paused. "I'm used to working on my own." It was the truth. Hayden Moore worked alone in his truck, providing for his mom, trying to take care of the house. He didn't ask anybody for anything, because people always let him down anyway.

"Well, let's team up this time, for Jane?" Clark asked.

Hayden looked back up to see Jane was gone from the doorway, but after hesitating, he gave in. "Okay, Clark. Show me the plan."

Clark led Hayden back into the pet store. L.T. walked at Hayden's heels, nudging his hand with his nose and licking his fingers. Stroking the top of the loyal pooch's head, Hayden walked into the backroom behind Clark.

Five guys sat around a big circular table, sharing a platter of tacos and pitcher of sweet tea.

"We can't install cameras sitting in here," Hayden said.

"Sit, eat," Jane said. Her hand lightly touched his shoulder blade and felt electric. Turning, his eyes met hers and he found himself frozen in that moment. When she turned her head and walked around the table, his eyes followed her.

"Are you going to eat with us?" Clark asked.

Hayden's head snapped in Clark's direction, and he nodded. Pulling a black folding chair back from the table, he took a seat. The man to his right passed him a couple of paper towels and the man to his left pulled the platter of street tacos toward him.

"Grab a few. They go fast." Jane's charming smile lit up her unique eyes.

Hayden couldn't break his gaze away from those eyes, even if he wanted to. Jane turned her attention to Clark, asking about the cameras. Thankfully she seemed unaware of the effect she had on Hayden, and he was glad for that.

He scooped two street tacos off the tray, but when he realized how small they were in his hand, he reached for a third just as the guy to his left started shoving the platter back toward the center of the table.

"Good call," the guy said. "I'm Roscoe. How do you know Jane?"

Hayden searched the circle of guys, and Jane, but no one was paying any attention to him and Roscoe. He spoke quietly, ducking his head so just Roscoe could hear him. "I'm Hayden. I was here the day she was robbed. I wasn't sure she would put up cameras, so I ordered them on my drive back to Oklahoma. I'm out here every week."

"Oh, you're the truck driver?" Roscoe nodded and turned to the table. "Guys this is Hayden. *The* truck driver."

"Oh, you were here that day?" Clark asked.

Jane's endearing smile turned back toward Hayden, and he averted his eyes before he found himself staring again.

"He was here. He didn't want to leave until the police arrived and everything. He even gave a better description than I did." Jane's voice was lyrical and warm.

"I'm a people watcher. I notice details, that's all," Hayden said.

"Do you haul out here very often?" Clark asked.

"Every week. This is my dedicated run. I usually stay at the truck stop outside of town, but I took an Uber to town because her pet store had good reviews on Google, and I ran out of dog food for this guy." He pointed to L.T.

"Bad day to run out of dog food," Roscoe said.

"Depends on how you look at it, I guess." Hayden looked across the table and found Jane watching him with her clear blue-green eyes. His face lit up in a warm smile and he studied her expression until she looked away.

"Once we're done eating, we have a camera to install back here, and then all the inside cameras are done. I think we should use the cameras Hayden bought outside, so the front and back door can be seen. Did I see that your security kit came with a motion sensor?" Clark asked Hayden.

"Three motion sensors and a glass break sensor for over the front window," Hayden said.

"Good. We should be able to rig it all together and then hook it up to the Wi-Fi so Jane will get alerts if anyone breaks in while she's gone, too," Clark said.

"I'm happy to help, but it's overkill, I think," Roscoe said. "We don't have this kind of trouble in Granby very often."

"But Jane deserves to feel as safe as possible. She was robbed at gun point." Clark crossed his arms over his chest and stared down Roscoe.

"Right, of course. We'll install all of it," Roscoe said.

"It should only take a couple more hours," Clark said.

"What do you want me to do?" Hayden asked.

"You can go back to that front corner and put up a camera. We'll do one on the opposite side, so they cross sweep the front door. We'll do the same on the back of the shop, too," Clark said.

Chapter Three

Jane

The early morning sun creeped over the horizon, turning the sky a multitude of colors— orange, red, pink, purple. The wispy clouds in the sky added texture to the colors, and the ocean, lapping gently at the sandy shore, reflected the brilliance of the picture overhead.

Jane walked near the water's edge, watching a small crab scurry out of her path. She heard the footsteps of a jogger approaching so she glanced up to see if she should scoot out of the way. Surprised, the jogger heading right at her was Hayden. She scooted left, away from the water, trying to avoid a collision with him. He had his headphones in and his phone in his hand, eyes on the screen.

His arm brushed hers as he passed and he whirled around, yanking his headphones out and holding his hand up. "I'm so sorry... Jane?" He grinned at her. "What are you doing out here so early?"

"I could ask you the same thing," she said.

"I love to run along the beach every time I'm out here. It isn't easy driving a truck and trying to be healthy, but it's important to me."

"Admirable." She pushed her long, black hair behind her ears.

"Do you walk out here often?" He jogged in place.

"Every day. Either before I open the store or after I close." She gestured down the beach. "You should go, I'm not trying to hold you up."

"I'm not in any hurry." He grinned with the right side of his mouth and Jane found herself thinking about how cute his lopsided smile was, recalling him making the same face at the pet store the day he helped with the cameras.

She looked down to his jogging legs and back up to his face. "You look like you're in a hurry."

"Trying to keep my heart rate up," he said.

"Just go, enjoy your run," she said. To make it easier for him, she turned and started her stroll down the beach again.

To her surprise, a few steps later, he was walking beside her.

"Maybe I could just walk today. If you don't mind me joining you?"

"I don't mind, but I don't want to slow you down, and I can't run the beach like you can," she said.

"Can't or just don't want to?" His tone was teasing, and he jutted out his elbow toward her.

She scooted away from the offending elbow and shook her head. "Can't. Seriously. I'm asthmatic. If I try to run down the beach, you're going to be dialing 9-1-1."

"We can't have two calls to the emergency department within the first thirty days of meeting each other, that would be bad. Real bad."

Jane covered her mouth and laughed against her fingers. She could feel Hayden staring at her and she glanced sideways at him. The intensity of his dark blue eyes held her attention until Hayden put his arm in front of her and said, "Whoa, don't step on him."

She froze and looked down. At her feet was a pink starfish and she smiled. "I love finding starfish on the beach."

"Sea Star," he corrected. "They have to be in the water. This one's washed up too far." Hayden gently scooped the starfish up and without regard for keeping his shoes dry, walked out into the water, bending down to keep the creature in the salty ocean current. He lowered it to the ocean floor once he was knee deep.

"You like starfish?" she asked as he returned, water dripping from his arms and legs, his shoes saturated.

"Yeah, I like them," he said.

"That salt water will be hard to get out of those

shoes. They look new, too," Jane said, appraising his shoes then meeting his gaze again.

"Oh, these old things?" He chuckled.

Jane continued strolling along the edge of the water. For a minute, she thought Hayden had parted ways with her. Thinking about looking back, she sucked her lip in between her teeth and closed her eyes. Her balance swayed and her eyes flipped open as she chided herself.

His footsteps caught up to her and he was beside her again. "Have you lived in Granby for long?"

"I was born and raised here. I've never left the state of North Carolina, and my trips away from Granby have been few and far between," she said.

His brow crinkled and his head tilted. Reaching out his hand, he touched her arm, bringing her to a stop. She turned toward him and their eyes locked.

"You've never left the state?" he asked.

"Not once. Not even as a child," she said.

"Does that bother you?" Hayden reached up and pushed her straight, shiny black hair away from her face. Their eyes had yet to move away from one another.

"Not really. I've never had a good reason to leave," she said.

"Family vacation?"

"I lost my parents a long time ago. I was married once." With this heavy admission, Jane looked back down the beach and started walking.

Hayden walked beside her, letting the sound of the splashing ocean water fill the void between them as they walked.

"I'm sorry," she whispered. Her right hand cusped her left as she moved along, head down, eyes on the sand.

"What happened?" he asked.

"Cliff died just a couple of years after we were married. Cancer. It was brutal." She stopped and turned to look out over the vast body of water beyond them.

"That's awful," he managed to say. He stood back, just out of her view.

Hayden

The warm April sun beat down on Hayden as he exited the Uber and thanked his driver. He pushed the door to the pet store open, L.T.'s leash in one hand, and two smoothies in a drink tray in the other.

"Hey, welcome back," Jane said.

"Hey to you, too. I need dog food for L.T. again and I thought I'd bring you an afternoon treat," he said.

"You didn't have to do that. It's good to see you, though." Her face lit up with a warm smile and it took everything in Hayden to peel his eyes

43

from her.

He set the drink tray on the counter by the register. "This one is oats, banana, dates, and cinnamon. And this is kale, avocado, green apple, and banana. Which one would you prefer?"

"Oats and dates and cinnamon." Jane grimaced at the green smoothie and a chill shook her shoulders. "Do you drink *that*," she gestured at the cup, "often?"

"I do. Green stuff is good for you." He twisted her cup free from the drink carrier and passed it to her. Then he twisted his out and tossed the drink carrier in her trash can.

"Can I give L.T. a treat?"

"Absolutely," Hayden said.

Jane came around the counter with a beef treat in her hand. "This stuff is practically beef jerky. I'm impressed with the ingredients and the price, so let's see if the pups like it, too." She knelt in front of the drooling white boxer and held the back of her empty hand out to him. He sniffed it and wagged his tail. Soon, his whole body was wiggling, and he was doing a funny walk-dance with his spine in a c-shape. She offered him the treat, which he took gently and then gobbled down.

"I think he liked it," Hayden said.

"He's so adorable. You got him as a puppy, right?"

"Yep. I think he was only five weeks old, but the people told me he was six weeks old. He had a hard time with dry food when I brought him home."

"Why didn't you crop his ears or dock his tail?" She raised a brow and he felt as though she was judging what he said next.

"Cost. Risk. There's no point in it, you know? The people I got him from didn't know much about breeding dogs. They were just a couple of friends who decided to get their boxers together and have a litter of puppies. He was the runt of the litter, and he picked me immediately." He rubbed L.T.'s head and stroked his back.

Jane nodded her approval before walking over to the shelf with his dog food. "The Earthborn Holistic in the blue bag, right?"

"You can remember what dog food I bought one time a month and a half ago, but you couldn't tell the officer what the guy was wearing when he robbed you?" Hayden laughed.

Jane pinned him with her eyes, but mirth was evident in the smile that was creeping across her lips. "What can I say? Pets are my life. I've run this pet store for more than twenty years."

"Do you have kids?" he asked.

Her head jerked and she froze in place. Slowly she shook her head from side to side. "No. You?"

"Nope. Never been married. Being a truck driver isn't exactly the kind of life that works for lasting relationships." He watched her as she came around the counter and set his dog food down. "I'm going to give him a bath while we are

45

here. That shampoo did wonders for his skin."

"Good. That's why I stock it back there." She lifted her smoothie up and took a drink from the straw. Her eyes brightened. "That's actually good."

"You don't drink smoothies?" He laughed again.

"You can't come in here laughing at me all the time, Hayden Moore. No, I don't drink smoothies. I've never understood why someone would want their food blended together in a cup. I'm not a baby or a senior, yet."

"But you can pack a lot of nutrients in a smoothie," he defended.

"Not if it looks, smells, or tastes like I bet that," she flapped her hand toward his cup, "tastes. Go wash your dog." Her last words sounded bossy, and Hayden didn't dare disregard them.

He took L.T. to the self-wash and told him, "In." The dog obediently climbed the ramp and stepped into the tub. "What is it with this lady? I like her, probably more than I'm supposed to," he said as he scrubbed the dog's neck and back.

"Fresh towels, right out of the dryer," Jane said. She gave Hayden a sideways glance.

His cheeks flamed red, and he didn't look up from scrubbing L.T. "Thanks," he mumbled.

Chapter Four

Jane

Sunday, the one day that Jane let herself close the pet store, and the one day she ate breakfast at the cafe. She sat near the window, soaking in the streams of sunlight that washed over her, while she waited for her skillet to arrive.

She held a book in one hand and a hot cup of tea in the other. Her eyes traveled the page left to right in a comfortable rhythm as she made her way down the left page, then started at the top to read the words on the right page.

"Fancy seeing you here," Hayden said.

Jerking and rattling her cup of tea, she lowered her book, and looked up at Hayden. "Don't you usually get here on Thursday and leave on Friday?"

"Are you stalking me, Miss Everly?" Hayden lowered a brow, giving her a playful, but pensive look.

Jane rolled her eyes. "Hardly. I'm not the one interrupting someone's reading."

"I'll go then," he said. Disappointment laced in his tone, Hayden sunk back, taking a step away from the table.

"Wait," she said. "You can sit, if you want."

As if he was afraid she might change her mind, Hayden took one long stride and sunk quickly into the chair, rocking it up onto two legs haphazardly before settling it back on the floor properly.

"So, why are you in town on a Sunday?" Jane put a bookmark in her book and closed it, then she dropped it down into a book cozy and then into her purse.

"Read much?" he asked.

"Only on Sunday," she said. "You didn't answer me. Are you avoiding my question?"

"What if I am?" he teased.

Jane looked up to meet his eyes and even as the server slid her skillet in front of her, she couldn't make herself look away. She cast a sideways, "Thank you," at the young woman.

"I'm not avoiding your question," Hayden lowered his voice, "my truck broke down."

Jane rubbed her fingers against her palms and tore her gaze away from his. Her pulse threaded along at a rapid pace, and she felt breathless. She tried to collect herself, tried to tell herself to breathe in slowly—she had enough practice coaching herself through asthma attacks that this should come easily. It didn't. She wanted to look up but didn't want to be locked into the enchantment of his gaze again. Or did she? Why did her feelings about this man feel like the beginning of a war inside her?

He should be just a customer that happened to meet her on the worst day of her store ownership. But she felt this draw to him. He felt comfortable and it was easy to talk with him. She stirred her skillet around, sucked her lip in, then drug it out of her teeth slowly. Steam rose from the plate in front of her and while it smelled delicious, she found her appetite waning with the butterflies that filled her stomach.

"I'll be here until at least Wednesday," Hayden said. "But I should be back in Oklahoma with my mom, she has another treatment this week."

"Treatment?" Jane's gaze lifted and she met his deep blue eyes, and just as she suspected, she found herself locked in what felt like the best staring contest of her life.

"For lung cancer. Let me tell you, chemo doesn't feel like treatment. It feels like torture, and I'm not even the one going through it," Hayden's voice was soft, entwined with pain as he talked about his mom.

Jane choked down a thick lump in her throat, dropped her fork across her skillet, and tried to swipe the tears that came faster than she expected. She turned to look out the window, desperately trying to hide the emotion that was

49

overcoming her. She didn't want to turn this moment about his sick mom into something about her or her dead husband. She could no longer remember just how Cliff's arms felt wrapped around her or how his voice sounded in her ear, but she knew their love was real and she still missed him.

"What stage?" Jane asked through her tears, still looking out the window and pressing her index fingers into the soft flesh just under her eyes.

"Stage three. She's been fighting for a year now," Hayden said.

Jane knew that wasn't good news, but she also knew there was enough doubt when battling cancer that sitting across from a naysayer was enough to drive anyone mad. She'd faced that in her former mother-in-law the sicker Cliff got. "I'm sorry." The words felt weak as they left her mouth and she silently prayed for something more meaningful to say.

"You said your husband died from cancer, when we were on the beach?" Hayden asked.

Jane nodded slowly and turned back toward the table. She stared down at her skillet, knowing full well that she wouldn't be able to eat a bit of it. "Cliff. He had pancreatic cancer. It was a terrible surprise and it all happened so fast. He died on our third anniversary," Jane said.

"That's terrible, I'm sorry," Hayden said.

Hearing him say the same apology she'd

uttered just moments before made her feel better for coming up short. She knew God had used that tragedy in her life, but it wasn't to give her elegant prose for someone else in her shoes. Maybe it was simply the way she understood. Maybe words came up short when hearts were broken.

"I think I'm going to head home now," Jane pushed her chair back, "Sunday is the only day I get to play with my dog and clean my house."

"I wondered if the pet store lady had any pets," Hayden mused, leaning forward and catching her eye.

She stopped sliding her chair back as her eyes met his. She couldn't help but wonder why she felt locked in place every time their gazes reached one another. "Bentley, a Yorkie. He's seven years old."

"Housebroke?" Hayden looked skeptical.

"Actually, he is. But I know that's hard to accomplish with Yorkies."

"My mom has one, she is about the same age, and she is not housebroken. I kind of hate that dog."

Jane laid her hand on her chest and turned her head away, finally breaking the hold his eyes had on her. "I can't believe you just said that," she teased.

Hayden laughed and pushed his chair back. "Do you live far?"

Jane crossed her arms and rose from her chair. "Some things are better kept secret."

Hayden

"It's just dinner," Hayden muttered, with L.T. at his side. He hung off to the side of the pet store, trying to convince himself to go in and ask Jane out for a bite after work. He pinched the tip of his nose between his thumb and crooked forefinger, then slid his fingers away, a nervous habit he'd had for as long as he could remember.

L.T. yipped at him and wagged his tail, curling his spine in that familiar c-shape and doing his little dance. Hayden shook his head. "I know, I'm all nerves for nothing," he said.

Pushing the door open, Hayden hesitated when he saw Clark at the counter talking with Jane. It was too late to back out, the door chimed—three pleasant cat meows, which set L.T. to barking and looking around at full attention.

Jane laughed and the sound was musical. While Hayden made an attempt to calm L.T., he thought he'd rather hear her laugh forever than settle the dog down. The thought stopped him short, and he skirted around the aisle, pretending to browse the shelves while he chided himself for thinking something like the word *forever* in regards to a woman. Forever doesn't work when you're a truck driver and you're never home.

Jane's smile and the silky smoothness of her long black hair came to mind. He thought of her crying at the cafe and how badly he wanted to hold her in his arms and shield her from the world. He ran his hand over his short strawberry blond hair and watched as Clark left out the front door.

"Don't tell me you need dog food already." Jane walked around the aisle, landing a hand on her hip.

"Don't need dog food. That was Clark, right?"

Jane nodded. "Pastor Clark. Just stopped by to make sure I was still getting a clear signal from all the cameras and sensors."

"He's a pastor?" Hayden was surprised by this news.

"All the guys that helped put in the cameras were from church," Jane said.

"I knew you said you'd get guys from church to help you, but I've never known church folk to be... helpful." He shrugged.

L.T. nudged a bag of treats and knocked it to the floor.

"If he slobbers on it, you have to buy it." Jane swiped the bag from the floor and shook it in Hayden's direction. L.T. sat on his haunches, his big brown eyes intent on the bag of treats. Jane tore the top off and opened it, giving him one of the pieces.

"You can't just give him whatever he wants, he'll end up acting like a spoiled brat," Hayden said.

"My store, my rules."

My dog—"

"Eh. My store. My rules." Jane pinned him with a hard stare and Hayden just nodded and raised a hand in surrender.

"Are you busy tonight?" Hayden asked. He reached up and pulled a bag of treats toward the front of the shelf, making the row even again.

"Not after I close the store for the evening, why?" Jane fed L.T. another treat from the bag in her hand.

"Would you like to go to dinner?" He meant to say it with more confidence, but his voice was feeble, and his mouth went dry on him.

"We could do dinner." Jane was so... nonchalant. What did that mean? Should he ask if it was a date or just let it rest? It had been at least two years since he took a woman out and he felt rusty. And here before him stood a woman unlike any other, he wanted to do this right.

"How's seven?" He choked out.

"Sounds good. There's this cute little bed and breakfast down by the coast. They've got great food and outdoor seating. It's so nice today I—"

"Outdoor seating and great food sound perfect," Hayden said.

"Perfect?" Jane raised her eyebrow at him and then laughed—that beautiful, musical laughter that Hayden was falling in love with.

Chapter Five

Jane

While the day before she'd lost her appetite over breakfast and worrying about Hayden's mom, she was ravenous during dinner and Hayden kept making her laugh.

"Did you fine folks save some room for dessert?" The boisterous, plump woman returned to their table.

"Oh, I don't know, Grace. I think I'm stuffed to the brim," Jane said.

Grace turned her back to Hayden and raised and lowered her brows at Jane, giving her a thumbs up. Jane's cheeks turned pink, and she covered her mouth, shaking her head.

"I don't usually indulge, but I'd love a slice of pie, what do you have?" Hayden asked.

"Strawberry-rhubarb or apple, sugar," Grace turned back even so she could see Hayden, too.

"Strawberry-rhubarb is my favorite," Hayden said.

"Have you had Jane's strawberry-rhubarb pie? This doesn't hold a candle to that divine slice of heaven." Grace grinned.

"Shhh. Don't tell him all the town secrets," Jane said.

Hayden tilted his head, studying Jane's expression. "You'll have to fix me up with one of your pies to take home to Mom. She loves strawberry-rhubarb, too. Better yet, why don't you come meet her?"

What was he saying, come meet his mom? Jane glanced up at Grace whose grin had grown in the last thirty seconds, and she shook her head. "That's insane. I can't leave the pet store."

"Ainsley can run it for you. School lets out in two weeks," Grace said.

"Hush, woman," Jane said.

"Who's Ainsley?" Hayden asked.

"My daughter," Grace said proudly, "and she works a few evenings and on Saturdays for Jane. She knows all the ins and outs. She'd be fine."

"What if—"

"No if," Grace interrupted Jane, "that man ain't comin' back and if he does, Ainsley's a smart girl. She'll hand over the money and send him on his way. She won't try to play hero. I already talked to her about it. But c'mon, Jane. Nothing like that happens in our town, ever. Stop worrying about it."

"See, Ainsley can watch the store, and you can come back to Oklahoma with me to bring Mom a pie. In a couple of weeks. I leave out Friday, I'm back by the next Thursday."

"No dessert?" Grace asked Jane again.

"No, thank you," Jane said.

The woman sauntered away, tucking her notepad back into her apron, and disappearing into the kitchen.

"You've already said you've never left North Carolina. It would be your first adventure out of the state, and my mom would love to meet you."

Jane folded her hands in her lap and leaned back. She looked away from the table and pursed her lips together.

"No, no. Don't do that. Don't shut down. We were laughing and having so much fun," Hayden said.

"Hayden," she turned toward him, serious, "I do have fun with you. I like you. But I can't get involved with someone who isn't here. This," she motioned between them, "can't be anything other than dog food at the store and a bite to eat because you're broke down."

"It's not like I'm proposing," Hayden said. Regret flinched in his face. "I didn't mean it like *that*."

"You're right. It's not a proposal. But it is next level, I'd say even scrious if I'm going to ride across the country with you and meet your mom. And I can't. I know what I can do and what I can't do. I can't do long distance. I can't worry about you six days while you're on the road. If it ever did become a proposal, I can't marry someone who can't be here to hold me every night. I'm just not the girl for the gig."

"It's not a gig," Hayden defended.

"I'm sorry," Jane said. "Enjoy your pie." She rose from her chair, folding her napkin beside her plate and grabbing her purse. When he tried to speak again, she held up her hand, shaking her head. "Have a good night, Hayden."

Hayden

Small, nearly swallowed by the rocking recliner she occupied, Hayden's mom sat with her shawl pulled close around her and a white, lacy surgeon's style cap on her head. He knew, hidden under the fabric, were the ravages of chemo and a bald head.

"Hey." He scooted a chair close and sat across from her.

He told himself he could handle his mom being sick, he could even handle her being taken from this world, but what he couldn't handle was watching her fade and become diminished. His already torn heart cracked a little further.

She lifted her head from the corner of the chair

where she'd been letting it rest to offer him a faint smile. Returning her head to its resting position, she stared out the window.

"I think I'm going to take the week off," Hayden said.

"Why? What about that woman you've grown so fond of?" Her voice was hoarse, nothing like the sweet voice he'd grown up hearing.

"She doesn't feel the same," Hayden said.

Despite the effort it took, she lifted her head again to look at him, narrowing her gaze. "You asked her directly? Or you're making an assumption?"

"You taught me better than to make assumptions," he reached out a hand and drew her hand into his, "I took her to dinner and asked her some questions. She made it clear that she isn't interested in a truck driver or the demands this job places on my time and location."

"So that's just it then, you're giving up?" Although her voice was hoarse, it was pointed, and he smiled seeing that his mom still had some of her fire.

"What is there to do? She lives in North Carolina, not here. It's not like, even if I found something different to do, I can be here for you and pursue something with her."

"So? Go live in North Carolina. I'm dying," as she emphasized the word dying, she started coughing. Yanking her hand from his, she covered her mouth as the coughing fit overcame her.

Hayden rose to his feet, laying a hand on her back, he reached over for her glass of water. When the coughing finally subsided, he handed her the glass. Her hand shook as she took it, sipped delicately from the glass, and then handed it back to him.

"I'm not leaving you, not any more than I have to. If I'm going to rearrange my life and career choice, it's going to be so I can live here, with you."

His mom rolled her eyes and waved him off. "I'll have no such thing. My grown son, living at home. I don't think so. You've been good to me, and you've had me your whole life. If you think you love this woman, you need to pursue her."

"What does that even mean? If I love her? How could I possibly know that?"

"Well, I know it. You need to catch up with the program. You can't stop talking about her. That's something. I've never seen you so captivated by someone. Not in forty-five years of being your mother. You're also not taking a week off to fuss over me. I can't have that. It makes me feel ridiculous."

Hayden froze. He'd never considered how she felt about his fussing over her because he had no idea what else he was supposed to do as she grew more and more ill. "Fine. I won't take a week off. But it's over with Jane. I tried and she was not interested."

"Hayden, I need you to listen to me. Sit down,"

she said. Her voice was hoarser since the coughing. Adjusting in her seat, she turned to fully face him. "I'm exhausted and the treatment is not working. I don't have long. I want you to live and love and enjoy your life. I do wish I'd had the honor of having a grandchild before this condition took over, but even if that happened tomorrow, I wouldn't live long enough to meet him or her. Stop wasting your time in this stuffy sick room. This isn't the place for a healthy young man to spend his days." She sunk back against the chair with a thud and let her eyes close as she tried to steady her rapid breathing.

Hayden sat across from her, too stunned to speak. The treatment wasn't working? He knew she was fading, but being faced with her certain, and probably not too far off death, was more than he could bear. Tears brimmed his lower lids and as hard as he tried to fight them, they spilled over and rolled down his cheeks.

Chapter Six

Jane

Not even sure if she was at the right truck stop, Jane eased her little car around the building to the truck parking. What was she thinking? She didn't even know the name of the company Hayden worked for, let alone the color of his truck. All she knew was, ever since she left him at dinner, she couldn't stop thinking about him. Every time she prayed, she felt it impressed on her heart to pray for Hayden's mom, a woman she'd never met, and whose name she didn't even know.

She came around one truck and headed down another row, looking from cab to cab. It struck her that the drivers lived in these spaces, and she was essentially looking into their bedrooms and invading their privacy. She gripped the steering wheel tighter, telling herself it was okay because it was daylight, but it was becoming harder to keep looking into each semi.

She saw motion and looked up, watching a man in a cap stroll from the building, across the parking lot, as he grew closer, she recognized his profile and scooted her car up. Rolling the passenger window down, she pulled up closer.

"I was beginning to think you weren't here," Jane said.

Hayden looked up, the sun lighting up his face under the brim of his cap. His eyes were red, and he looked exhausted. "I didn't expect to see you anytime soon."

While his words stung, she knew he wasn't wrong for thinking it, and she nodded. "I shouldn't have left dinner like I did."

"We were down to dessert anyway." He forced a lopsided smile and rested his forearm on the frame of the door, leaning down into the car slightly.

"I made this," she lifted a pie from the passenger seat, "for you and your mom."

Hayden's eyes averted then, and he muttered, "Thanks." He accepted the pie from her hands.

"What's wrong?" Jane asked.

"The treatment is not working," Hayden said, still not looking at her.

The words hung heavy in the air and Jane put her car in park. She knew what it meant when cancer treatment wasn't working. Who is ever ready for those words? That loss? She gripped the steering wheel and stared out her windshield. "You didn't come here to hear me cry about my mom. I'll tell her it's from you." He glanced her way, lifted the pie in thanks, and pushed away from the car.

Jane turned her head in time to see the back of him as he walked away from her car. She pushed open the driver's side door and rounded the rear of the car. "Wait, Hayden."

He stopped but he didn't turn around.

"What's on her bucket list?" Jane asked.

Hayden's head tilted and slowly he turned to face her. "Bucket list? She's too sick to get out of her chair."

"When the chemo stops, she'll feel better for a few days. At least, that's what happened to Cliff. The doctor warned us not to get too excited, but we made the most of the days he felt good. You should find out what she wants to do when she gets all the energy and feels good. It won't last, but better to make memories while you can. At least, if it was me in her shoes, I'd rather use that energy than sit around waiting for it to burn out."

She realized then she wanted to go to him, to wrap her arms around him, and instead of wishing for someone to hold her again, she wanted to hold him in the middle of this deep pain. The rumble of a semi as it rolled by tore her from her thoughts and she considered what a man on the road really meant. It was still too much, but she took a step toward him, then another.

When she reached him, she wrapped her arms around him and hugged him. His embrace was powerful, overwhelming even, and she thought it felt like he might never let go. Maybe she didn't want him to let go, ever.

Hayden

Sprinting down the beach as fast as his legs would propel him, he saw her before she was ever aware of him. The sun was just peeking over the horizon and light was spilling over the beach, washing everything in the hazy light of early morning. Sitting in a chair, with her toes just out of the reach of the lapping ocean water, Jane sat with a book in her lap.

Hayden considered just running past her in the hopes that she'd still be there on his way back so he could speak to her before he left Granby, but then it dawned on him that he might miss his chance if she'd left the beach while he finished his run and made his way back to her.

As he slowed, she turned her head, her clear blue-green eyes taking him in. The warm morning breeze blew her straight black hair back from her face, and an affectionate smile tugged up the corners of her lips. He bent just a few feet from her chair, clasping his thighs and gulping in deep breaths of oxygen.

"Good run?" She laid her hand on the open page of her book and twisted her body in her chair.

"Running on the beach is my favorite." He sunk to the sand beside her chair, propping his arms on his knees to look out over the water. "L.T." He cupped his hands around his mouth, yelling for his companion.

"Did you talk to your mom?"

"I did. It was hard asking her what was on her bucket list, and it's even harder accepting that making it happen immediately is necessary, or she might not live long enough to fulfill her wish."

"What's her wish?"

Bounding around the rocky corner beyond Jane, L.T. came back, panting and exuberant. Hayden cradled each side of the dog's face, making incoherent sounds at him, and then pushing him away. Leaping into Hayden, the boxer knocked him onto his back and licked his face. Once he righted himself, Hayden cleared his throat. "She wants to see the ocean. She's never been."

"There's a lot of ocean to see," Jane said. "Does she have a specific beach or location or something about the ocean she wants to see?"

"She wants to see a sea star in its native habitat, and she wants to swim in the salty water," Hayden said.

Jane sighed and turned her gaze out over the

water. She smoothed the open pages of the book in her lap without looking down. "How do we get her to the ocean then?"

"She had her last round of chemo two weeks ago. I was hoping you could give me some insight." Hayden's voice came softer as he spoke. L.T. settled onto the sand next to Hayden, laying his head in his owner's lap.

"I have no idea." Jane closed her eyes, opening them again she lifted one shoulder in a slow shrug. "I can't remember when Cliff's last chemo was and when he got his burst of energy."

Hayden thought about asking what they did, but that felt too personal. He thought about confirming that she really loved the man, but that seemed too obvious. He stroked L.T.'s head. "What are you reading?"

She tapped the pages and smiled, but she didn't turn her head toward him. "The Bible."

"Do you read it a lot?"

"I try to read it every day, but I miss some days."

"You really believe the stuff in that book?" He raised a brow in her direction.

Jane bowed her head, staring down at the words on the page in front of her. "With my whole heart," came her whispered reply.

Hayden never knew such a soft reply could hold so much conviction, but he knew for certain that she did believe the Bible. "Why did God take your husband? Why is He taking my mom? And with cancer? Why torture them to death?"

Jane

Why? It was the one answer she never really could get her head or her heart around. Even all of the church rhetoric around a greater purpose, God's plan, a fallen world, why was something she couldn't ever put her finger on. She found herself wanting to give Hayden a flowery, poetic response to his question. She wanted to give him an answer that would make him see how great God really was, but she felt lacking as she held her Bible in her lap and dug her toes in the soft, moist sand just out of the ocean's reach.

"Jane?" His voice hung heavy with the question in the space between them.

She turned slowly, adjusting her weight onto her hip, and closing the Bible in her lap. She leaned onto the arm of the beach chair and rested the side of her face against her hand. "I don't know. I know that's not the answer you want. It sure isn't the answer I want to give. But God gives and God takes away and He is God. I asked why for a long time. But that changed over time to how do I use this pain? How will He use this pain? How is my story being impacted this way going to make the world better? I know He never left me. He sent comfort and peace and people to love me and carry me through the years," she said.

It felt like a small answer to such a big question, but it was the truth.

"Like the church people putting cameras up for you?" Hayden asked.

"In the beginning it was meals. I didn't have to try to feed myself for the first month after I lost Cliff. God sent people with food. People from church, people I never met. Then it's been fencing projects, painting, repairs. You name it. Someone always shows up and I see Jesus in them, in their actions."

"Good people do things for others even if they don't know Jesus," Hayden said. He turned his attention away from her and back to L.T., who rested his head in Hayden's lap.

"I'm sure they do. Most of the people that live here love Jesus. But I know a lot of people put forth humanitarian effort without loving Jesus, without even knowing Him."

"But you think God sent the people to your life that helped you?" Hayden asked.

"I know He did. He's orchestrated the smallest details that couldn't have been consequences. They were the hand of God. And I've been deep in the throes of grief and felt the peace that surpasses all understanding. It didn't mean I was happy to have lost so much. But I knew God was with me," Jane said.

"The church wasn't so helpful to Mom and me.

It was just the two of us growing up. My dad... he was an addict and he hurt my mom a couple of times. We have no idea where he is now. I don't even remember him. She reached out to a couple of local churches for help, at least a time or two, and was turned away, or chastised for having a child with no husband around. No one took the time to find out that they were high school sweethearts, that she married him three years before I was born, or that he'd hospitalized her once because of the way he hurt her." Hayden pried a rock from the sand and chucked it into the ocean.

"You know, the church doesn't always get it right. It's full of sinful people. They didn't become perfect because they accepted Christ. Christ is the only perfect man," Jane said.

Hayden stretched his arms behind him, palms down, propping himself up. The sun had risen higher in the sky and the air around them was warming. "Do you have to get to the store soon?"

"I do," she said.

"I need to get back to my truck. I've got to take your pie to my mom and figure out how to get her to the ocean."

"Do you think you'll bring her here?" Jane asked, a hopeful tone threading through her sweet voice.

"I think so," Hayden paused. He glanced up at Jane then back out to the ocean. Inhaling deeply, he turned back to face her. "I think you should tell her about Jesus the way you know Him."

Chapter Seven

Hayden

"Mr. Moore, I need to advise you that traveling when she feels better is not a great idea. She will take a sharp turn downhill, and it will likely mean that her passing is imminent. You wouldn't be near to me, to her other doctors, the hospital she is familiar with," Dr. Waterman said.

"Correct me if I'm wrong, but isn't dead here the same as dead somewhere else? If she's going to die, and you can't do anything about it, why can't she die somewhere she's having fun and she's at peace?" Hayden folded his arms over his chest.

Dr. Waterman looked over Hayden's shoulder at the closed door behind them. Just on the other side, his mom waited for him. "Listen, you don't have to understand, but I know from experience, it's comforting to patients, and their families, to have familiarity during those last days and hours. You don't want some stranger, that you have no relationship with, speaking doctor gibberish at you as you sort through your feelings and sit at her bedside while she dies. Here, we can comfort you in her final hours. We can comfort her. We know what medications she tolerates and which ones she doesn't. It's for the best, really," Dr. Waterman sounded firm.

"I don't buy it. If she isn't afraid to die under a different doctor's supervision or at a different hospital, then I'm taking her on a road trip like she asked me to."

"You could shorten the time you have with her. Wearing her out will make her body and immune system weaker." Dr. Waterman tapped her pen on her desk, staring Hayden down.

Hayden thought to throw the awful effects of chemo in the woman's face, but none of this was really her fault, anyway. He shrugged. "We'll figure it out as we go. Thank you for everything, Dr. Waterman." Hayden pushed his chair back from her desk and left the room.

Linking arms with his mom, he patted her hand. "Ready to go home?"

"What did Dr. Waterman say about a road trip?" she asked.

Not being able to lie to or deceive his mom, he detailed the conversation to her as they walked the corridor to the elevator, rode down to the parking garage, and walked over to his pickup truck.

"What it comes down to, Mom, is whether you care if you are here or somewhere else when the energy fades and it's the end," Hayden said. His voice and expression were solemn, and he faced her with a question in his eyes.

"Dead is dead, isn't it?"

"That's what I said to Dr. Waterman."

"Then let's hit the road Jack, we ain't never comin' back." The mirth in her voice reminded him of days past.

The smile plastered on his face was for her benefit and contradicted all the fear and doubt clawing through his mind and shredding his heart.

Hayden

"Are you sure your boss didn't care if you took a little time off?" Mom asked as she climbed into the front seat of the RV.

"I'm sure. They understand," he said.

"So where did you get this thing?" She gestured behind her toward the rear of the RV.

"Do you remember Dave? From school?"

"How could I forget? You two were inseparable," she said. Maple jumped up and put her paws on his mom's leg, giving a little whimper.

"It's his. When I told him what we were doing, he offered it up. Said it would be more comfortable and allow you to rest more during our travels than that pickup of mine would. I had half a mind to argue with him, but he was right. This will help me keep you comfortable," Hayden said.

"What's our first stop?" She gripped the handle above the window with her frail hand.

"I'm going to take you on my route, which eventually takes us to the ocean. You've always said you wanted to see the trek I take to and from North Carolina. Well, I'm going to show you. And we'll eat at all the best places on the way there and back." Hayden fired up the engine and then turned to take in his mom's expression. The delight in her eyes told him all he really needed to know.

"Does there have to be a trip back?" she asked.

Hayden laughed. "You're funny, Mom."

"You didn't answer my question. What is our first stop?"

"I'm thinking Memphis, TN. I'm sure we'll stop at a gas station or two along the way. But we could spend a night or two in Memphis and look around the town."

"I'm not interested in seeing Memphis," she said.

"Well, we are eating there. It's non-negotiable. But we don't have to stay there."

"How will we get around the towns we do stop in? This thing is a beast."

"Well, my original plan was to use Uber. But Dave put his scooters in the back for us."

"In the back?"

"Yep. This fancy ol' thing has a back area that once we unload the scooters, functions as a deck of sorts."

"Fancy-shmancy. What about Maple and L.T.?" She lifted the little yorkie into her lap and rubbed her head, making kissy noises at her.

"I brought a crate for Maple, so she doesn't pee in Dave's RV. And L.T. will just lay down and nap while he waits for me."

"Do you think he will tear anything up?" She glanced back at the boxer as he walked toward the rear of the RV.

"Never does in my truck. He's used to road life, remember?"

"Will I get to meet this girl of yours?" There she went, changing the subject. He wondered when she was going to ask about Jane.

"I don't have any girl other than you, Mom," Hayden said.

L.T. paced the aisle of the RV, nudging his nose into Hayden's arm and then pacing again.

"Nonsense. I want to meet Jane before I die. I want to know if she's the right woman for this stubborn man child I raiscd. It isn't right that you've never settled down or taken a wife."

"We'll see, Mom," Hayden said. He rolled his eyes and backed the RV out of the driveway. He'd hoped that meeting Jane could be a surprise, but it was too obvious telling her they were headed to North Carolina. Of course, she would want to meet the woman who'd captivated him.

Jane

Jane's cell jingled in her pocket as she and Bentley strolled along the beach. She fished it out and smiled when she saw Hayden's name across the screen.

"Hey." She stopped walking and turned to look out over the vast expanse of the Atlantic Ocean.

"Hey yourself. Things go well at the store today?" Hayden sunk back into the red camping chair he occupied, just a stone's throw from the camper.

"Business as usual. How far have you made it?" Jane continued her stroll along the coastline.

"Not far. Little Rock. I thought she'd be up for a better pace, but she's worn out. You were right though; her energy has returned. I haven't seen her this exuberant in months."

"That's good, at least. There's a starfish here—"

"Sea star," Hayden corrected.

"Sea star here on the beach. Should I put her back in the water?"

"Is she all the way out?"

"Yes, out of reach of the low tide," Jane said.

"Take her out until you're knee deep in the water. But Jane, set your phone down so you don't lose it in the ocean." He leaned his head against the back of his chair, and he closed his eyes. He could smell the salty air and feel the give of the sand beneath his feet. He loved the beach. Even brighter in his mind was the image of Jane, scooping up a sea star and returning it to the ocean. He waited for the sound of her voice to break into his reverie.

"Okay, she's back in the water, safe and sound," Jane said, slightly breathless.

"Are you okay?"

"I'm good," she turned the phone away from her face as she huffed wheezy, short breaths. "I just ran too fast in and out of the water." Bentley bumped her leg with his black nose and gave a little yip.

"You weren't kidding about your asthma." Hayden's head shot up. He stared off across the campground. Tension knotted the muscles between his shoulder blades and up his neck as his imaginings turned from bliss to Jane being alone and not able to breathe.

"No. It's no joke. I really can't run even ten feet. But I can walk a long time." She straightened her body as her lungs calmed and her breaths came easier.

"Are you out there alone?" Hayden's voice was stiff with worry.

"It's just me. I'm okay. I have an inhaler with

me if I need it," Jane said.

"I'm hoping we make Memphis tomorrow. I'm going to take my mom to get my favorite fried chicken if we do," Hayden said.

"I like good fried chicken." Jane eased herself onto a bench along the beach and watched the sky change colors as the sun eased down behind the horizon.

"You're going to have to get out of that little town one of these days and let me show you the world," Hayden said.

"Or maybe you're going to have to get out of that truck and try settling in one cozy place. It's not bad, you know."

Hayden

Hayden stretched his six-foot, two-inch frame out on the couch and then rubbed his eyes. L.T. stuck his nose in Hayden's face.

"You should let me sleep there, I'll fit better. Especially if you aren't going to fold it out into a proper bed," his mom said.

Hayden blinked his eyes several times and when his vision cleared, he pushed the nosy boxer out of his face. He stared over at his mom, sitting at the little table with two steaming cups of coffee and a box of Danishes. She sounded more like herself than she had in ages. He pushed himself upright and swung his legs to the floor. L.T. rushed him and landed in his lap, licking his face. Hayden pushed the dog down again, rubbing both sides of his face and his ears.

"I didn't want to make too much noise when I came in last night," Hayden said.

"Oh, don't worry about that. The medicine they gave me for sleeping works like a charm," she said.

"Do you think you need those now that you're not on chemo?"

"Hadn't thought about it. I guess I can see how I sleep without them. I got you coffee and a couple of apple Danishes." His mom bent down and scooped up Maple. The little yorkie whimpered and tucked her head up against his mom's neck.

"How did you manage that?" Hayden's eyebrows pinched together. He walked over to the table and sat across from her.

"The couple that is camping here and keeping the place cleaned up are just the sweetest. I took a little stroll and when I told them I'd like to surprise you with breakfast, they were surprised we weren't traveling with groceries. But the wife offered to take me to town."

"You can't just ride to town with strangers, Mom."

"They were sweet, I knew I wasn't in any danger. Besides, I'm your mother, not your child. Eat something and don't gripe."

"How are you feeling?"

"How does it look like I'm feeling?"

"Pretty good, I'd say. If you've been out for a walk and gone for breakfast. Did you save enough energy for traveling?"

"Let's get this show on the road."

Hayden

Two hours later, Hayden and his mom crossed over the Mississippi river bridge, into Memphis, Tennessee.

"There's a lot to see here," Hayden mused.

"Ocean, son. Take me to the ocean," his mom said.

"We're getting our lunch here." Hayden brought the RV down a street that seemed barely big enough to accommodate it, but he managed to find a vacant lot to park the oversized vehicle in. Adjacent to the empty lot was an old building, with a yellow sign that read, "Gus's World Famous Fried Chicken" hanging above the entrance. The green door needed a coat of paint, and it didn't quite look like they were open.

The aroma of fried chicken and spices saturated the air around them.

"Smells good," his mom said.

"Do you want to sit over there with L.T. and

Maple while I go inside and order?" Hayden asked.

"Wait... what are you going to get me?" His mom raised a suspicious eyebrow.

"Fried chicken, that's all they serve. I thought I'd get us both a breast and a sweet tea. I'll get yours regular, but I like the spicy."

"Oh now, I can't do spicy. It tears up my stomach after all that chemo," his mom said.

"I know, that's why I'll get yours regular."

"C'mon," she whistled at the dogs, taking L.T.'s leash from Hayden's outstretched hand. The little yorkie trotted alongside the white boxer. L.T. looked back at Hayden with his sad brown eyes.

When Hayden pulled open the door the place came alive with warm, friendly greetings.

"Dining in?" His usual waitress grinned at him.

"Outside with the dogs, like always."

"Of course," her southern drawl was thick, and she winked at him, "how many pieces today, dear?"

"Two breasts for us to eat now. And then a breast and a thigh to-go," Hayden said.

"You got it. Sweet tea?" She scribbled on her notepad.

"Two, please," Hayden said.

"Mmhmm. You got it, honey." She looked a little disappointed that he wanted two teas this time. She sashayed past Hayden and disappeared between two swinging doors.

He went back out the same faded green door he entered through. Sliding into his chair across from his mom, he took L.T.'s leash and patted the panting boxer on the head.

"How did you find this place?" his mom asked.

"I saw it on a show. There's a good barbecue joint in town. More than one, I'm sure. But one that I eat at every so often."

"I like barbecue," his mom said.

"I know, but this is the better of the two, promise."

"I trust you," she said. "How was Jane last night?"

"Fine," he said.

The waitress came out the side door, one sweet tea in each hand. When she reached the table, she gave one to his mom first. "One for the lady." She turned to Hayden, her grin widening. "One for the gentleman. And since you're always in here alone, are you going to tell me who this lovely woman is?"

Hayden smiled at the waitress, then at his mom. "Beatrice, this is my mom, Shelly. Mom, this is Beatrice. She's here every time I stop in."

"How often do you eat here?" his mom asked.

"On almost every run." Hayden laughed.

"That is too much greasy fried food. You're going to have a heart attack," his mom said.

"Oh now, Miss Shelly. Look at him," and Beatrice did look at him, from head to toe and back again, "Hayden takes good care of himself. Running and working out when he's stopped every day. A little fried chicken is good for his soul."

Shelly shook her head and laughed. Hayden turned his head, his cheeks turning a little rosy.

"I'll be back with y'alls chicken, alright? Don't go nowhere," Beatrice said. She sauntered away, glancing back over her shoulder before disappearing into the building.

"Thank you," Shelly called after Beatrice. His mom leaned across the table and spoke with a low voice, "I think the waitress likes you."

Hayden waved off his mother's words. She'd spent the last twenty years trying to find someone, anyone, to hook him up with. He pictured Jane sitting by the beach with her Bible and felt an unfamiliar tightness in his chest. Every time he thought of that woman, he felt a new emotion. Something locked away was coming to life. He wondered if he should be taking his mom half-way across the country to meet Jane, or if he was making the biggest mistake of his life.

Chapter Eight

Jane

Bentley sat at Jane's feet, looking up at her expectantly. She loved his soft brown eyes, always looking for the next treat. After she finished ringing up the woman at the counter, she bent down and gave her happy companion another beef morsel.

"Who's a good boy?" She rubbed the top of his head and rose to her feet again.

The speaker behind her made a cawing sound, like a parrot had been let loose in her store, and she looked over to the door.

"Welcome to the Granby pet store. Can I help you find anything?" Jane asked.

The woman entering was older, wearing a homemade surgical style cap adorned with bright flamingos and palm trees. The blazing sun obscured Jane's view out the door, but it looked like someone was holding the door for the woman. A little yorkie trotted alongside the woman, scurrying into the building and looking cautiously up at her owner.

"Your shop is lovely," the woman exclaimed.

"Thank you. I'm Jane. If I can answer any questions—"

"I do have one question," the woman interrupted, a sly smile spreading across her aged face. "How do you feel about my—"

"That's enough, Mom," the familiar voice Jane had been waiting for all morning finally tickled her ears.

"Hayden," Jane came around the counter, Bentley on her heels, his leash drawn through one of her belt loops.

"Jane, this is my mother, Shelly. And Mom, this is Jane," Hayden said.

Jane wanted to hug the man standing before her, but then she thought maybe that would be too forward, so she hesitated her step and stuck out her hand, offering to shake his.

With a puzzled look on his face, he shook Jane's hand. Jane turned to Shelly with her outstretched hand. Shelly lifted one eyebrow and smirked. "I'm not that kind of mom." She wrapped her arms around Jane and gave her a long squeeze.

Jane melted into the woman's warmth and hugged her tightly. "It's so good to meet you, Shelly. Hayden speaks so highly of you."

Shelly only stepped back half a step, and she

cupped Jane's face in her hands, peering into her eyes with an inquisitive nature. Jane held still. While Shelly's expression was inquisitive, Jane felt like she was being sized up, judged.

Dropping back next to Hayden, Shelly turned her head to catch his ear. "She's lovely, son."

Jane's cheeks flamed red. She knew the words weren't meant for her ears, but she was glad for the positive assessment. "I only have about twenty minutes left before I close the store. Are you hungry?"

"Starving," Hayden said.

"I don't know how you eat what you do and retain this figure of yours." Shelly poked her finger into Hayden's ribs, causing him to laugh. "I'm hungry too. Now that I think about it," Shelly said. "I got so used to never being hungry. I've eaten more on this trip than I had the whole last six months."

"You've got your color back, too." Hayden stared at his mom for a moment.

"And my energy. I can't wait to get down to the beach," Shelly said.

"You brought her here before you took her to the ocean?" Jane's eyes grew wide.

Hayden's head swiveled and he smiled warmly at Jane. Those eyes of his, and the way his lips parted, revealing his white teeth including a sneaky jagged tooth, made butterflies flit about in Jane's stomach.

"I wanted you to go with us," Hayden said.

Jane nodded, at a loss for words, she ducked behind the counter again and told her computer to run her end of day report. She felt like an intruder in Shelly's special moment, but she wanted to be there, she wanted to be next to Hayden. She feared the coming days would be hard as Shelly's energy faded and her illness became evident. She shook her head, trying to dislodge the thoughts from her mind.

"You okay?" Hayden asked, standing very near.

She turned toward him, her big blue-green eyes brimming with tears. She blinked, wondering if it would be better to wipe the tears away or pretend they weren't there. "I'm fine."

"Did I do something?" He reached his hand forward, letting his fingers graze her arm and then his thumb wiped an escaped tear from her cheek.

"No," her voice came out soft, broken.

Hayden pulled her close and wrapped his warm arms around her. She let her head rest against his shoulder, and she heaved a sad sigh into him as he held her. She'd long come to accept that life was often filled with opposing emotions but this war between the love growing in her heart and the grief over the love she lost so many years ago was fierce.

Jane glanced past Hayden, seeing that Shelly was perusing the aisles and paying them no attention, she pulled back from Hayden just enough to see his face. "I hope her energy and color last a long time. This all just brings back memories for me. I won't be a big ol' crybaby the whole time."

Hayden's hand slid up to her face and his thumb wiped another tear away. "You can cry. I won't tease you for it. I shouldn't have brought her here, I'm sorry."

"Oh no. Don't say that." Jane squeezed him with her arms, feeling his squeeze in return, she smiled at him. "I want to know her. I'm just not good at hiding my feelings."

"You don't have to hide them from me," Hayden said.

Hayden

Hayden hung back a few strides from his mom and Jane. His focus never far from the two women as they strolled the beach, bumping into each other, laughing, and pointing out critters in the sand. The smile on his mom's face was enough to make him happy, but coupled with the smile on Jane's face, Hayden felt overwhelmed with joy.

"Look! A starfish," his mom said. She picked up the pace and hurried over to the small, five-armed creature.

"Sea star," Hayden muttered behind them.

"She needs to go back in the water," Jane said.

"Really?" his mom turned to her, with wider eyes. "How do we do that?"

"Just scoop her up and carry her out until you are knee deep in the water," Hayden said.

His mom looked down at her capris and tennis shoes, her pursed lips squished to the left side of her face as she considered everything. "Can I take my shoes off?"

"Yep," Hayden said.

Jane stood to the side, watching the two of them. Hayden flashed her a sweet smile. When his mom took her shoes off, Jane reached for them.

"You don't want sand in your shoes," Jane said.

"I guess I should have worn my flip-flops, too," his mom said.

"You were in too much of a rush to get down here to listen to me." Hayden chuckled.

Reflecting glints of light off the surface of the ocean, the sun hung above the horizon, still beating hot waves of light down on them. His mom scooped up the sea star and cradled it carefully in her hands. She dipped it into the water as she entered the ocean, getting it wet again. She waded deeper in the clear-blue salt water and laughter rose up from within her. She bent over, lowering the sea star into the water, not letting go until she could gently set her on the ocean floor.

When his mom straightened, she was facing away from him and Jane, and she held her arms out wide, soaking in the sunshine and squishing her toes in the sand.

Jane averted her eyes, looking out toward the horizon. Hayden watched Jane, knowing she was, in her own way, giving his mom space to enjoy this moment. Jane wrapped her arms around her body and inhaled a deep breath. Hayden stepped closer to her. He wanted to put his arms around her, but he wasn't sure if it was the right moment, so he grazed the back of his hand slowly along the length of her arm.

She sighed and turned her head, a sweet smile tugging up the corners of her lips. "It's lovely out here this evening."

"It's perfect," Hayden said.

Jane leaned to the side, letting her shoulder meet with his.

"I'm glad you're here." He draped his arm over her shoulders and squeezed.

She turned into him and wrapped her arms around his neck. "I'm glad you brought your mom here to see the ocean."

Hayden slipped his other hand around her and hugged her. "Me too."

Lost in the moment, gazing into Jane's lovely blue-green eyes, Hayden missed the sound of his mom wading back toward the beach. But he didn't miss the sound of her sweet laughter just before she patted him on the back. "This answers all my questions."

Like sheepish teenagers, Hayden and Jane pulled back from one another. Hayden shoved his hands in his pockets and Jane gazed out across the water.

"Oh, don't stop on my account, *that* was fixing to turn into a kiss." His mom flapped her hands toward them, shooing them toward each other, yet neither of them budged.

"What questions did you have?" Hayden eyed his mom suspiciously.

"I just wanted to know what was happening between you two, exactly." She lowered herself to the sand and sat cross-legged, looking up at Hayden with a wry smile.

Hayden pulled a hand from his pocket and gestured toward Jane, giving her the chance to answer his mom for them.

Jane shrugged, a little chuckle escaping her. "He drives a truck and he's only here once a week. I don't know how to make something out of so little. I don't do long distance." Heat rose to her cheeks, and she swayed, casting her gaze out over the ocean again. She heaved a sigh as tears wet her lower lashes.

His mom clicked her tongue. "That is a problem. Sounds like some problem solving needs to happen, and soon. Before he lets a good one get away." She narrowed her gaze at Hayden, staring at him with a serious expression.

Chapter Nine

Jane

Jane enjoyed spending a week strolling the beach with Shelly and Hayden, even going so far as to take two days off from her pet store. Ainsley was happy to get the extra hours and Jane was so proud of how well the young woman handled the store.

"Was seeing the ocean everything you hoped for it to be?" Jane asked as her and Shelly took a seat in camping chairs near the water's edge.

"I never want to leave." Shelly's words were thick with emotion and Jane reached out to squeeze her hand.

Hayden built a circle with stones and then gathered sticks and a log to make a small campfire. "It would be nice to stay here forever."

"We should," Shelly said.

Jane turned her head from Hayden to Shelly, a

flicker of hope growing in her heart. It was a lot to ask of him—to leave his truck, his work, the life he'd been living behind. While she had vocalized her frustration over his coming and going, she hadn't asked Hayden to make a change. But she couldn't help thinking of their future if he did settle in Granby.

"We can't just stay here, we have to take the RV back," Hayden said.

"So, you take the RV back. Then drive back out here," Shelly said.

"What about your house?" Hayden asked.

"Let's be honest, it's yours now. So, what about it? Do you want it? Do you want to sell it? There isn't anything in that house that I can take with me, or that I need for my last couple of weeks on this earth." The resolution in Shelly's voice caused Jane to grow tense.

"But Shelly, what if you have longer than that?" Jane asked.

The woman chuckled and shook her head. "Not even all your praying is going to buy me extra time, sweetheart. And even if, by some odd chance, I lived longer than a couple weeks, coming to terms with my own end has made all the stuff I've accumulated seem rather worthless."

"Mom," Hayden turned from the fire to face her, "don't talk like that. Let's roast hot dogs and enjoy s'mores for our last night on the beach, and tomorrow we will take the RV back to Dave and check in with your doctor."

Shelly gripped the arm of the chair she sat in, bunching the fabric in her hand. "I'm not leaving Granby. I've already talked to a man about a rental, and once he heard my plight, he agreed to rent to me month to month so long as I keep the house in good repair. Which I obviously will do. I want to die here, where the air smells salty and the critters run back to the water, and the sunrise and sunset reflect over the rippling surface of the ocean. I don't want to die in some hospital bed, or even my stuffy old bedroom."

Hayden lit the fire, muttering something under his breath as he fanned the flicker until it turned into a flame.

"Where is the house you're going to rent?" Jane asked.

"Three doors down from you, neighbor." Shelly's face split in a wide grin, deepening the wrinkles at the corners of her eyes.

"Thomas's place? That's great. He's a good man," Jane said.

Hayden smoothed his palms over his shorts as he remained squatted by the fire. "Mom, you can't just move here like that. That's weird."

"At least I'm not too afraid to do what I want to do," Shelly said.

Jane's cheeks flamed red. The conversation felt like it was taking a personal turn and she felt like an intruder. She looked out across the hazy horizon. The sun, having just disappeared from sight, still lit the sky and sent a brilliant array of colors spanning out over their heads and to the other side of the world.

"I don't know what you're implying." Hayden stood and crossed his arms, staring at his mom.

"Just that you know what you need to do and you're too scared. It wasn't a very hidden meaning," Shelly said.

Jane stood from her chair, glancing between the dueling pair, and then walked down the beach. Having left her sandals by her chair, she felt the sand squishing between her toes, and she inhaled the salty ocean air deep into her lungs. Whatever Shelly was getting at felt private, and she wanted the two of them to work it out without an audience.

She ambled along until the stars twinkled overhead and the sunlight was gone. Pausing to take another deep breath she turned to meander back toward the fire that appeared to lick the sky in the distance. A shadowy figure passed between her, and the fire and she startled.

"Hello?" She squinted into the darkness.

"Why did you leave?" Hayden asked, his hand reaching for hers.

A shiver ran down her spine from the startle and from his sudden nearness, but she let him have her hand.

"I just thought you and your mom needed a minute," she said.

"Thanks." He squeezed her hand and brought it to his lips, kissing the back of her fingers one by one. "Jane?"

She waited, but when he didn't go on, she gently cleared her throat. "Yes?"

"How do you feel about my mom moving three houses down from you?"

"It doesn't bother me in the least. I can help look after her, too. Plus, everyone in town is great. And I know you wanted me to talk to her about Jesus, but I haven't felt the Holy Spirit's prompting yet. I've been praying for the right moment. And for her to have more time."

Hayden raised his other hand and cradled the side of Jane's face. She let her eyes close for a moment as she listened to his quiet breathing.

"Are you sure it isn't weird for you?"

"It's not weird at all. I admire that she knows what she wants," Jane said.

"What do you want?" Hayden asked.

You. The only thought that came to Jane's mind, but she held back, not sure if she should say that to him now.

Chapter Ten

Jane

Jane waved to Pastor Clark as he parked in front of Shelly's new house. The big box truck rumbled until he killed the motor, and then the street grew quiet as usual. She crossed the yard and opened the wood gate, sticking a wedge under it to hold it open.

"We've got some nice stuff for Miss Shelly," Pastor Clark said as he came around the back of the box truck.

"I'm so grateful. You always come to my rescue," Jane said.

Robin, the pastor's wife, hopped out of the passenger seat of the box truck. "Hey Jane. Any more trouble at the store?"

"None, thankfully." Jane rested a hand on her hip, watching as Pastor Clark lifted the back gate of the truck.

"That's good to hear," Pastor Clark said. With the gate up, he lowered the ramp and then climbed up it into the truck. "We have a couch, a chair, a dining table with four chairs, a double size bed, and a dresser."

"Excellent. Shelly is at breakfast with Hayden for probably the next hour. Let's see if we can get this unloaded and set up for her," Jane said.

"Hold your horses little lady, let Roscoe get here to help me. You and Robin can carry in some of the smaller pieces, like the lamps and whatnot," Pastor Clark said.

"Lamps?" Jane raised a brow and climbed the ramp into the back of the truck.

"And end tables, and a nightstand. He didn't give you the whole list. We also brought towels, dishes, and later, we will be by with freezer meals and groceries," Robin said.

"You didn't have to go to so much trouble. I just wanted her to have a few pieces of furniture to get started," Jane said.

"Of course, we did." Robin reached out and squeezed Jane's arm. A knowing look passed between the two of them. Robin was the only person Jane had enlisted to pray for Hayden and Shelly's salvation.

Jane hoisted a lamp up against her shoulder and then lifted a sack that was behind it. Robin followed with an end table and another sack. Pastor Clark remained in the box truck, undoing the ratchet straps and wrapping them up neatly.

By the time Jane and Robin came back outside, Roscoe had arrived and was helping Pastor Clark haul the mattress out of the truck.

"We'll just get this in and lean it on the wall, then we'll get the box spring. Once we set up the frame, we can put the bed together," Pastor Clark said as they passed the women.

"We got her some really pretty sheets. A blue fleece set, my favorite. And a mint green bamboo set. That way she has colors and textures to pick from. There's a comforter, too. It's brown and looks nice with either set of sheets." Robin led the way back up the ramp into the truck. She grabbed a chair for the dining room table, so Jane did the same.

Hayden

Hayden eyed the box truck parked in front of his mom's house as he held the gate open for her. She led the way up the walk to the front door, digging in her purse for her keys.

"Breakfast was delicious, thank you," his mom said as she turned her key in the deadbolt. "Weird, that didn't feel locked."

Protectively, Hayden reached around his mom, holding the doorknob. "You wait out here." He twisted the knob and as it clicked open, the scurrying people inside froze and stared right at him. Jane, Pastor Clark, Roscoe, and a woman he was unfamiliar with stood in his mom's living room. The night before, the home was empty, and his mom had commented that she'd have to figure out some furniture for her last few weeks.

Now, the living room had curtains, a couch, a chair, an end table, and a bookcase. As he pushed the door open and waved for his mom to go past him, he could see a table in the dining room with four chairs around it.

"What have you done?" His mom's voice was demanding as she stared straight at Jane, but the playful smile on her lips told him she was pleased.

"Furnished your home," Jane gestured around the room, "with help, of course."

"This looks lovely," his mom said.

"Shelly, meet Pastor Clark, his wife Robin, and Roscoe," Jane pointed to each one. "Guys, this is Shelly, Hayden's mom. Oh, and you haven't met Robin yet, have you?" Jane turned toward Hayden with her brow raised.

"I haven't." Hayden stepped forward, outstretching his hand to shake Robin's, then shaking Pastor Clark's hand and then ending with Roscoe's. "This looks great. I can't believe you guys did this for her."

His mom leaned close to Jane after making her introductions. "I'm not a penniless old hag, I hope you know. I was going to find some pieces. It's just that Hayden already has so much to worry about with my home in Oklahoma. I didn't want him to have a bunch here. But this is where I want to spend the last of my days."

"Mom, it's fine. Don't worry so much," Hayden said.

Jane wrapped her arm around his mom's shoulders and squeezed. "And all of this stuff, unless you want to do something else with it, can go back to the church to help other families when they need it."

Robin held up a hand. "But let me make it clear, this stuff is yours. So, if it doesn't come back to the church, we won't be hunting you down."

"Hard to hunt down a dead woman," his mom said.

While everyone else in the room sucked in a breath and froze at his mom's words, Roscoe started laughing.

"That's the truth," Roscoe said, slapping the side of his leg.

Robin and Jane led his mom through the house, showing her what they'd done in each room.

"I'm going to head out, boss," Roscoe said, clapping Pastor Clark on the shoulder.

"Sure thing. Thanks for your help today," Pastor Clark said.

"Yeah, thanks a lot, man," Hayden said.

"Anytime," Roscoe said.

Hayden had heard people say that many times in his life. Anytime. He rarely, if ever, thought it was a genuine offer, but as he watched Roscoe walk out and thought about how these two had helped Jane after the robbery, he was convinced that Roscoe really meant it. What made a man decide to do so much for others?

"Jane said you're headed back with the RV today. It's already Wednesday, so I'm guessing you won't make it back in the big truck until next weekend?" Pastor Clark pulled out a chair at the dining room table and sat down.

Hayden followed him, sitting across the table from him. "Yeah. I'll get this back to my buddy on Friday. Work on Mom's house over the weekend, and then start my run Sunday night."

"Do you stop other places?" Pastor Clark asked.

"Depends on what my load is. Sometimes I come straight up here, but other times I deliver and pickup multiple loads on the way. But I have a load that picks up every Sunday up here, so that's how they work out my loads. It's all around that pickup," Hayden said.

"So, they've had someone else doing it for three Sundays now?" Pastor Clark pushed his glasses back up his nose.

"Yep."

"Have you thought about moving here with your mom? At least for the time being?"

"The doctor said she only has a few weeks. We've already used up a week of that time. I don't know about moving for such a short time. And I've been with Trans-Con for fifteen years."

"That's a long time," Pastor Clark said, nodding his head slowly. "There's more than just your mom here, you know?"

"Yeah," Hayden muttered.

"Jane's here," Pastor Clark said.

Hayden propped his elbow on the table, looking past the Pastor, out the window over the kitchen sink. His mind wasn't focused on the view because he was picturing straight, silky black hair, clear blue-green eyes, and a sweet smile.

"I know of a job opening for a truck driver. If you're interested," Pastor Clark said.

"Doing what?" Hayden turned his attention back to the pastor.

"Delivering stuff to pet stores and feed stores. It's regional. Home every night. Benefits. Good pay," Pastor Clark said.

"I'd have to unload at each stop, right?" Hayden asked.

"Yes, but they make it worth it," Pastor Clark said.

Hayden held up his hand and shook his head. "I'm not afraid to do the work. I was just asking. When do they need someone to start?"

"Immediately, but they could wait a couple of weeks for you to wrap up loose ends," Pastor Clark said.

"How do you know so much about the job?" Hayden raised a brow.

Pastor Clark chuckled. "My brother owns Statewide, a distribution warehouse. We're pretty close and I mentioned that I might know someone looking for work."

"Why?" Hayden pulled his head back a bit, a puzzled look etching across his face.

"Because when Jane told me your mom wanted to stay, I thought that might inspire you to stay, too."

His mom poked her head around the corner. "Are you trying to inspire my son to stay in Granby?"

"Mom," Hayden sounded stern, "not now."

She lifted her hand and waved it through the air. "I'm going to town with Jane and Robin. When are you leaving in the RV?"

"Soon," Hayden said.

"Well, then give your *not now mom* a hug. I'll see you next weekend," she said.

Chapter Eleven

Jane

Arm-in-arm, Shelly and Jane walked out of the auditorium. Shelly's eyes were wet with tears. "Do you really believe this Jesus stuff?"

"With my whole heart. I don't know how people go through this life without Jesus." Jane patted Shelly's arm, then reached for a tissue from the box on the banister.

"I haven't ever felt so loved somewhere. Or so cared for. And when Pastor Clark was speaking about Jesus... he made him sound so... so real." Shelly sniffled and accepted the tissue from Jane, dabbing at her eyes.

Robin came out of the auditorium, and seeing the two ladies huddled together, she moved over to them and wrapped her arms around them both, whispering a prayer that, while Jane couldn't make out all the words, she heard her *amen*.

"Hey," Shelly said. "I was just asking Jane if she really believes all this Jesus stuff."

"I do," Robin said. "He's pulled me out of the clutches of addiction, he saved my son, and because of Jesus, I am never alone."

"Addiction?" Shelly blinked wide eyes at Robin.

"Yes. Addiction. I was a drug addict when I was seventeen. But Jesus set me free," Robin said.

"I want to have Jesus in my life," Shelly said.

Enthusiasm bubbled up and Jane squeezed her, giving an excited, "Hooray!"

"I can pray with you," Robin said.

"I would appreciate that," Shelly said.

"Just repeat after me." Robin bowed her head and led Shelly in a salvation prayer.

Jane bowed her head and praised the Lord for His goodness.

When Shelly lifted her head after the prayer, her eyes were wet with tears and she released Jane to squeeze Robin, then it was Jane's turn. As the three women talked in an animated fashion, Pastor Clark approached.

"Hey Pastor," Jane said during a lull in the conversation.

"Hey, everyone looks awfully happy here," he said.

Robin told him about Shelly's decision, and he wrapped Shelly in a warm hug. "Welcome to the family."

"Thank you. You all really do make it feel like a family around here. I've never experienced that before." Shelly reached like she might push her hair behind her ear out of habit, but all she had was a little fuzz, concealed under a baseball cap.

"Have y'all talked to Hayden today?" Pastor Clark asked.

All three of them shook their heads, with Shelly asking, "Is something wrong?"

"Oh no." Pastor Clark shook his head. "He just called and at first I thought you might be celebrating his news."

"News?" Jane asked.

"Yep. The real estate agent had an offer on your house the same day it was listed." He looked at Shelly, then to Jane. "And he's going to stay here in Granby for a while."

Jane's cheeks reddened as the smile on her face spread. She was surprised Hayden didn't call her or his mom first, but then she couldn't blame him. At least for not calling her. She'd been back and forth with her feelings about him. Wanting him, but not wanting to get involved with someone who was gone so much. She imagined he felt confused. Besides, he was probably only moving to Granby until his mom... she couldn't even bring herself to think about what was coming right then.

Chapter Twelve

Hayden

Hayden parked his pickup truck in front of Jane's store and checked his reflection in his rear-view mirror. Jane hadn't been around since he got back from Oklahoma, except for stopping by one evening with meals for the freezer, and a study book for his mom. His mom had been pouring over the Bible every waking moment for the last several days.

He pushed open the door and the chime made the sound of a sheep. Hayden's eyebrows scrunched and when his eyes found Jane, he asked, "Do many people have sheep as pets?"

"I like to change the noise, otherwise it gets old," she said.

"But seriously, what do you sell here for pet sheep?" He shoved his right hand in his pocket and walked toward her.

She was straightening items on a shelf, and she laughed. "Nothing for sheep here, sorry to tell ya."

"Well, that's a shame," Hayden said.

"How's your mom today?" Jane asked.

"Doing great. When I left the house, she was on the back porch taking in the view and reading her Bible."

Jane nodded.

"How are you?" Hayden wanted to reach for her, but she seemed distant, and he didn't want to make her uncomfortable.

"Good." She pulled some dog treats forward, but her eyes moved toward him several times.

"We're going to cookout today, for the fourth of July and all. Want to come eat with Mom and me?" Hayden shifted his weight to one leg and then back to center.

"I'd like that." She turned more toward him. "I think it's really great you are here to support your mom. I was afraid, with your job and all, that she might," her voice dropped to a whisper, "die alone."

"You wouldn't ever let that happen." Although an alarm in his head said he shouldn't be grinning at her in the ridiculous way that he was, he couldn't help the smile on his face. It just grew wider and wider.

"You're right, I suppose." She turned back to her work, dusting and wiping the shelf and pulling products forward.

"I know it's weird that she's sick and now I'm

staying with her, which feels ridiculous at my age, but I didn't just come to Granby for her."

Jane turned toward him again, color rising in her cheeks and making her even prettier. Her eyes widened just a little bit, and that hopeful smile tugged at her lips. The urge to hold her grew and he took a step toward her.

"I understand why you don't want to start something with someone who is gone all the time. The truth is, the more I'm around you Jane, the less I want to be anywhere else. But I'm here now. Can we see what this is between us?"

Jane stepped toward him, the hopeful smile giving way to a joyful grin. Her clear green-blue eyes met his and he saw affirmation there before she spoke. "I'd like that. I just need you to know something. I'm not *that* kind of lady. I've never been with anyone but my late husband... if you know what I mean."

While he couldn't claim quite the same purity she had, he'd always driven a truck and he thought those things were for committed relationships, of which he'd only had a couple. "I'm not looking for *that*. I want you. I want to walk the beach with you and watch the store with you. I want to hold your hand. I want to talk with you and learn more about you. I want to love you, Jane. For the rest of our lives," Hayden said. He stepped closer still, and this time he pulled his hand from his pocket, and he reached for her. She slid into his embrace and rested her head on his shoulder.

"I want to love you, too," she whispered into his ear.

Jane

Shelly sat in a chair at the water's edge. The lapping sea licked at her bare toes and Jane watched her curl them into the sand from time to time. In Shelly's lap lay Maple, sound asleep. Cradled in her arm was her Bible, and she poured over the words, rarely looking up.

Jane stood at a table, her own bare feet in the sand, slicing tomatoes. "Those burgers smell good."

Hayden stood over the grill he dragged down on the beach, making sure to keep the charcoal hot and flipping the burgers, chicken, and hot dogs as he needed to. "We should have invited Pastor Clark and Robin. And Roscoe, too."

"They are probably at one of the grills along the shore, doing the same thing we are doing." Jane pointed and across the beach, quite a way off, other families could be seen along the sand.

"Why is it so much quieter on this side?" Hayden asked.

"People think this is private. With our houses right here, everyone assumes this is owned land.

But you can't own the beach," Jane said.

"I have to admit, it's kind of nice having a private section though." Hayden flipped a burger, but it fell sideways between the grates. While part of it stuck up, the other part sat directly on the coals. Using his tongs, he pulled the patty up and turned toward Jane. "Can I get a plate?"

"You can't eat that." She wrinkled her nose as she pulled a plate off the stack and carried it over to him.

"You mean you don't want the patty with coal ash on it? Adds flavor. Character." A grin spread wide on Hayden's face.

The look of disgust spread on Jane's face, and she shook her head, making a *bleh* sound.

"Actually, I thought I'd rinse the ash off and let L.T., Maple, and Bentley share it," Hayden said.

"None for Bentley. His stomach doesn't tolerate a change in food." Jane looked back at her yorkie, who laid under the table she'd been working at, napping.

L.T. was tied to a tree closer to the house, but he looked anxious to join the cookout.

"Does he run off?" Jane asked.

"Nope, I just didn't know how many people would be down here. And he will steal food while we aren't looking. So, it's best if we leave him tied until we are done eating." Hayden set the plate with the ashy burger on the side table of the grill. "I'm about ready for the pan to put the meat in."

Jane grabbed the pan off the table and walked

it over to him. "I have the veggies cut up. Mayo, mustard, ketchup out. Pickles. Looks like you've already got the cheese on the burgers."

The setting sun sent a spray of brilliant colors across the evening sky. Pink, orange, red lit up the expanse of the heavens above them, looking almost like a fire had caught overhead. The dazzling sight reflected off the surface of the ocean, and Jane sucked in her breath.

"I've never seen fireworks over the ocean," Hayden whispered in her ear as he bent close and took the pan from her.

"It's the best," she said.

"Next year, you should come to the mountains with me. Fireworks in the mountains are spectacular, too."

"Like where?" Jane asked.

"Colorado," he said.

"It's really your goal to get me out of Granby, isn't it?"

"You should go with him. Wherever he wants to take you. There is something special about seeing the world. Don't wait until you don't have time, Jane. Don't be afraid," Shelly said. Her presence so near startled Jane, as she'd been entirely focused on Hayden.

"I'm not afraid," Jane said. "I'm comfortable. This place is home and I have roots and my store."

"Then let me run the store. You need an adventure in your life," Shelly said.

"You can't run the store, you're—"

"I'm what? Dying? Sick? Stop with that. I'm living my life. And until the good Lord calls me home, I'm here to stay. Besides, it would give me something to do," Shelly said.

"Mom, I meant next year for the fourth. To see the fireworks over the mountains," Hayden said.

"Fine, good. Plan other trips now. The sale on my house should be finalized in a couple of weeks. I was going to give you that money anyway. Sell your house in Oklahoma. Doesn't look like you'll need it anymore. This girl needs to see the world. Yellowstone, have you seen Yellowstone?" Shelly narrowed her gaze at Jane.

"I've never left North Carolina," Jane said.

"Never?" Shelly's head tilted to the side.

Jane shook her head.

"We can talk about this later. Let's just enjoy the holiday, eat some good food, and watch the fireworks," Hayden said.

L.T. whined and tugged on his leash, then dug his paws into the sand.

"He likes that idea. He's ready for some grub," Shelly said.

Hayden walked up and untied the dog's leash from the tree.

"What would you like on your burger?" Jane asked Hayden.

"I'm a big boy, I can..." he trailed off, focusing his attention on her.

Jane bit her lip. Acts of service was one of her love languages, but she wasn't trying to step on his toes.

"Mustard, tomato, and onion please," Hayden said.

Jane assembled the burger and reached into the bag of chips, but he made a funny noise and she looked up at him.

"No chips. I'll take some of the fruits and veggies, though," he said.

"No chips?" Jane scrunched her nose up.

"How do you think I keep this girlish figure?" Hayden waved his hand down his side and back up.

"Running, I believe." Shelly rolled her eyes at him.

"That and watching what I eat. Which is hard in a truck, for your information," Hayden said.

Jane scooped the cut-up pieces of fruit and the veggies onto his plate and then walked it over to him.

"No one's made a plate for me since my mom said I was big enough to make my own," he said. "Thank you."

She rubbed his upper arm and leaned close, whispering, "Get used to it if you plan on sticking around here."

A loud pop and a spray of bright flames lit up the sky in a lovely shade of purple.

"Oooo, they're starting!" Jane jogged back over to the table and assembled her burger, grabbed a handful of chips, called to Bentley and hurried over to her blanket. Several more explosions of sound and color lit up the sky and she clapped her hands.

She felt Hayden staring at her and she glanced over, the smile on his face made her stomach flip and she bumped her shoulder into his. "Can't a girl love fireworks?"

"But you didn't want me to buy any to set off ourselves?" Hayden questioned.

"Nope, I only like the ones that light up the sky," Jane said.

"That makes no sense," Hayden said.

Shelly's laughter could be heard from her chair, where she happily munched on a burger and held Maple in her lap.

"It doesn't have to, does it?" Jane asked.

"No." He pushed her long black hair away from her face. "It doesn't have to."

Chapter Thirteen

Hayden

Hayden backed his pickup truck under the camper trailer, using his hand on the back of the seat to help him twist around. Getting the camper centered over the hitch in the first shot, he hopped out of his truck with a grin. It was a short-lived grin, as his doubts returned. Having never been unemployed in his life, spending a few months taking Jane to different things and bringing her home to check on the store and his mom between stops was nerve wracking. Not to mention his constant, nagging fears that Jane would hate camping and traveling or that his mom would die while they were away.

Camping. He laughed as he patted the side of the camper and then dollied it down onto the ball in the back of his truck. When he brought up camping, he planned on a tent. In his mind, tent camping was real camping. But Jane seemed hesitant and then his mom found the camper for sale and insisted that he buy it.

Ten years old, it was in excellent condition, having been garage stored and only used for what looked like one- or two-family trips a year. The price was fair, too. And when the man selling it heard his mom's story, he dropped the price even further.

Hayden shook his head as he plugged in the lights. His mother always had something up her sleeve. He couldn't help but worry that she'd push too hard and frighten Jane. But the two seemed to have hit it off better than he ever could have hoped for.

"All set?" His mom came around the back of the camper.

"Food is all loaded, beds are made, dishes are secured. We have maps and everything. Do you really feel comfortable running the store?" Hayden asked.

"Of course, I do."

"You do remember that Jane was in the middle of being robbed when I met her, right?"

"And? It was the first and last time. Nothing is going to happen. You guys are only going to be gone for a week. Just see how she likes the road. Natural Bridge State Park is gorgeous." She rubbed the spot between his shoulder blades.

Jane came around the front of the truck, a black bag hanging over her shoulder.

"That's a big purse," Hayden said.

"It's not a purse, it's a snack bag. I thought it would be good to have a few things in the truck for while we are driving."

"I don't snack while I'm driving. Bad habit and even worse for the waistline," Hayden said.

Jane looked like she was about to roll her eyes, but she stopped herself and turned toward his mom. "Have you been to the Bridge Park?"

"You mean Natural Bridge State Park?" his mom asked.

Jane nodded.

"Sure have. When Hayden was fourteen. We camped there for a week, and then we spent a week in Old Stone Fort State Historic Park. We took long camping trips every summer until he got in that truck and drove away." Tears misted his mom's eyes. "I'm so proud of the man you are, son. So proud."

Jane tipped her chin and turned away. She casually wiped her eyes, but Hayden knew his mom's words made Jane tear up.

"Thanks, Mom," Hayden said. "You know, we were always going somewhere, camping, even locally. Why didn't we ever go to the ocean on one of our trips?"

His mom fixed her gaze over Hayden's shoulder for a long pause. She inhaled a deep breath, held it, then said, "The day your dad put me in the hospital, we were supposed to leave for a trip. He decided last minute he didn't want to go. I wanted to go anyway. I don't know why he snapped that day. But we were headed to Destin, to see the beach. It took coming to terms with the end of my life to regain the final bit of security he stole from me. But I was no longer afraid to say I wanted to go see the ocean. And I'm so, so glad I made it here before my time was up."

How was Hayden supposed to decide which woman to hug? His crying girlfriend who had listened to his mom with wide-eyed horror? Or his stoic mom, who lost so much, but fought her way back from the bottom of the pit? He couldn't decide, so he held out an arm to each of them and like a magnet, drew them in. He kissed the top of Jane's head and squeezed his mom tightly.

Jane

While the hike to the natural bridge in the state park had been a tough one, Jane was glad they set out on the adventure. The bridge was beautiful, and Hayden led the way up the path to the top of it.

"We can walk across it," Hayden said.

"Are you sure it's safe?" Jane asked.

"Yep." Hayden used his walking stick to help him with the climb. L.T. walked ahead of him, wagging his tail and sniffing everything.

Jane used her walking stick, too. Although she lacked the skill that Hayden displayed. "Do you hike a lot?"

"It's my favorite way to spend a weekend. Camping and hiking. I really wanted to bring you tent camping. Roughing it is the way to go. You know, my mom and I backpacked into some truly primitive camping areas sometimes. We would purify water, catch fish, small game. She can clean a rabbit or a fish rather quickly. And she knows just how to cook them over a campfire in her cast iron skillet." Hayden glanced back at Jane. "It gets really narrow here."

She craned her neck to look around him and saw the space between two rock formations. Steps had been carved in the path, but she shivered at the tightness of the space. "It looks like, at any moment, we could get crushed by these rocks."

"They are gradually moving away from each other, not closer together. It will take a long time, but eventually this will be much wider, until one of these formations falls away."

As Hayden reached the last step, he offered his hand to Jane.

She reached up and let him help her with the last couple of steps. The view from their side of the bridge was breathtaking.

"Like it?" Hayden nudged her with his elbow as she stared across the landscape.

"Love it," she said.

"Come on, let's go across." He entwined his

fingers with hers and led her toward the bridge.

"Are you sure?" She tugged on his hand and slowed her pace a little bit.

"Yes, I'm sure."

She nodded and followed behind him. L.T. continued leading the way, but he didn't pull on the leash. He happily sniffed at the plants and then the rock as they stepped on to the natural structure.

"If we continue on, we can ride the Skylift, if you want," Hayden said. "The views from it are spectacular."

"Sounds good, but can we take a breather?"

Hayden stopped. Concern etched in his expression when he turned to face her. But she smiled in a reassuring way.

"I'm fine. We've just been going for a while and you got excited and started walking faster," Jane said.

"I didn't mean to," Hayden said.

"I feel bad for holding you back. I'll never be able to keep up with your pace, my lungs just won't do it. But I'm sure glad that I made a habit of walking every day. I wouldn't have made it out of the camper otherwise."

"For someone with breathing trouble, you've taken good care of yourself. Don't feel bad. I like having you with me more than I like going fast." Hayden stepped closer, brushing his fingertips along her cheek.

Butterflies took residence in her stomach,

setting it to flips and flittering at the warmness in his voice and the tenderness of his touch.

"Thank you for getting me out of Granby. This trip has been incredible," Jane said.

Chapter Fourteen

Jane

Jane's sweetly familiar hometown came into view as they wound around a final curve in the road. With the passenger window down on the truck, she could hear the faint sounds of the sea slapping at the rocks at the bottom of the cliff. The bed and breakfast that greeted everyone as they arrived in Granby looked the same as always.

It felt comfortable coming home, and a sense of peace washed over her. She enjoyed the adventure, but she learned what she always thought was true: home was her favorite place to be.

"Can you drop me off at the store?" Jane asked.

"Why don't we both check on Mom, and then we can go unhook the camper and I'll cook something for dinner," Hayden said.

"I think it's my turn tonight," Jane said.

"I called it, so it's my night." Hayden made a side-to-side motion with his head which made Jane erupt in laughter.

"Whatever you say," she said.

Hayden parked along the curb of the side street and the two walked around the corner and down to the pet store.

Opening the door, Jane heard a jingling sound and looked down to see bells clattering against the glass. "Where's my door chime?"

"You mean the baa-baa black sheep sound?" Shelly cocked her hip to the side and rested her hand on it. "I disconnected it. I don't know how you tolerate that thing a hundred times a day."

"I don't think that door has ever opened a hundred times in a day," Jane said.

"Then you have an influx of customers, which explains why we are running out of things even though I've followed your order sheet to a T." Shelly motioned for Jane to follow her, and she showed her several barren spaces on the shelves. "The phone rings off the hook, too."

"I'm sorry," Jane said.

"Sorry?" Shelly cocked a brow. "Why on earth would you be sorry? This is a business. We want it to be busy. I figured out that this pet store was only on the Facebook, so I spent lots of time getting you a website, and on Google. Hopefully that will help keep this place busier. Even Ainsley was surprised by how many customers we had. And, for the record, you should post more on the

Facebook than you do." Shelly led the way behind the counter.

"It's just Facebook, Mom," Hayden said.

She waved him off and rolled her eyes.

Jane noted the triumphant look on Shelly's face and so she smiled at the older woman. While she didn't think her store needed to be all over the internet, it was important to Shelly, and she could tell it was an act of love and kindness.

"What's this?" Jane tapped an envelope that was tacked to the corkboard above her desk.

"It was taped to the door one morning when I got here to open the place up," Shelly said.

Scrawled with bad handwriting, in blue ink, were the words, "I'm sorry." Jane pulled the tack from the corner of the envelope, and she broke the seal, opening it up. Inside the envelope was money but nothing else. Jane counted the cash and she held it up, looking at Hayden with bewilderment on her face. "Six hundred and twenty-seven dollars."

"Isn't that how much the robber got?" Hayden asked.

"I think so." Jane counted the money again. Arriving at the same figure as the first time, she shook her head. "I've been praying for him. Praying for the Lord to convict him and also to set him free. Looks like God's been working on him."

"He should still face charges for what he did," Hayden said.

"Agree to disagree? I'm just thanking Jesus that

the young man had a change of heart," Jane said.

"What if it wasn't him? What if it was his mom trying to make amends on his behalf?" Hayden said.

"We'll never know," Jane said.

Hayden

The early morning sun was just starting to peek over the horizon, but it found Hayden and Jane sitting along the beach, a warm mug in each of their hands. Hayden's mug was filled with coffee, while Jane was drinking a cup of Earl Grey tea.

"Have you considered the future?" Hayden asked.

"I've always just taken things one day at a time, honestly," Jane answered.

"I mean for us, between us," Hayden said.

A smile spread on Jane's lips, and she turned her green-blue eyes on him. Warmth radiated from her expression. "Now that you've accepted Jesus, I think a future between us can be considered."

"The Jesus thing is a deal breaker for you, huh?" He tilted his head, studying her face.

"I didn't want to shove it down your throat, but it is a deal breaker. I can't do long term with someone who doesn't love Jesus," Jane said.

"I didn't get it at first, but watching you, my mom, and even the people from your church, it started to come together. Nothing was quite as powerful as when God got a hold of my heart though. I'm glad He didn't give up on me," Hayden said.

"Me too," Jane agreed.

"So, about future us. I don't want to act like we are running out of time, but I also don't want to pretend time goes on forever. I thought we'd been dating since the fourth of July, at least. But you made it pretty clear after I accepted Jesus was when the real *us* began. Which was just a few weeks ago." Hayden sucked in a breath and glanced out over the ocean. The water looked pink as it reflected the glorious sunrise taking place around them.

"That wasn't much of a question, I don't know what to say," Jane said, her voice soft.

"Right. My question, I guess, is how long do you expect me to date you before I can propose? And after I propose, how long do I have to wait to marry you, Jane Everly?"

Jane's hand went to her mouth, to cover the gaping hole where her jaw went slack because her brain was in overdrive. "Propose? Marry? Do you really want that with me?"

"Why wouldn't I? You are the best person to ever walk into my life. I don't want to rush you, but I'd marry you tomorrow if you'd let me,"

Hayden said.

"Tomorrow is too soon. What about six months?" Jane said.

"Six months to propose, or six months to marry you?" Hayden rested his elbow on the arm of his chair and set his chin on his fist, staring at her.

"Six months to marry me," she said.

"So can I propose now?" Hayden asked.

Tears dampened Jane's lower lashes. She slowly nodded her head and Hayden shot out of his chair, dropping to one knee in front of her, he reached for her hand. She willingly let him take it and he kissed the back of each of her fingers. "Jane, my love. The only woman I've ever loved the way that I love you. Would you do me the honor of becoming my wife?"

The tears broke free and trailed down her cheeks as she scooted forward in her seat, clutching his hand with both of hers. "Yes, Hayden. Yes, I would love to be your wife."

Epilogue

Two Years Later

Jane cradled a fussing infant in one arm, while she held her phone to her head with the other. "Yes, I think it's his ears again... We need to be seen as soon as possible... I'd rather not go to the emergency room... Four forty-five this afternoon? We'll be there... Thank you."

"I can't go with you that late," Hayden said as Jane set the phone down. "Tabetha has a ball game and it's an hour drive. We have to leave an hour before the appointment."

"It's okay, I can handle the doctor on my own," Jane said. "Do you want to take Scott and Sarah? Or should they go with me?"

"I'll take them to the ball field. Maybe they will start to open up a little bit." Hayden pressed his lips to his wife's forehead, and then he stroked the baby boy's head. "It's alright, Carl. Mama Jane will get you to the doctor today and you'll start to feel better."

"Do you want me to come to the doctor with you, Jane?" Shelly asked from the kitchen. She was busy cutting fruits and vegetables up and assembling snack bags for the kids to grab from the fridge.

"Would you rather have her help at the ballpark?" Jane asked her husband.

"Nope. Take her to the doctor with you. That way if your arms need a break, you have help. Hopefully it doesn't get any worse between now and then, but last time he was so miserable. Did you put cotton in his ears?" Hayden asked, reaching for the baby.

"I forgot about trying that. I'll grab the cotton balls." Jane passed the tiny boy to Hayden and disappeared down the hallway. As she went, she knocked on the kids' bedroom doors. "Come grab a snack!"

When Jane returned with the cotton balls, Hayden was leaning against the kitchen counter, holding the boy against his chest and covering his exposed ear with his palm.

"I think the air hurts them. I bet the cotton settles him down until the doctor gives him something," Hayden said.

Hayden moved his hand and Jane tucked cotton into the first ear, then after Hayden repositioned the baby, she tucked cotton into his other ear. He seemed calmer just that fast, and just in time.

Three teenagers descended on the kitchen like vultures, snatching up snack bags from Shelly. Only Tabetha said, "Thank you," in her sweet voice. The twins, Scott and Sarah, were too busy fussing with one another. Jane thought that at fifteen they should have outgrown arguments about whose bag had more in it, but that wasn't the case. They argued at every snack and meal about who got more.

Jane wiped her hand over her tired eyes and rubbed Carl's back as he dozed off in Hayden's arms. "I know we said no babies, but I was so glad when our case worker called about him. I really did want a baby in the house," Jane said.

Hayden peered down at the boy, then looked over at his wife. "I thought you were out of your mind for saying yes to him three days after the twins arrived, but I'm so glad he's here, too."

Shelly patted each of their forearms. "I'm so proud of you two. Foster care is so important. And I thank God every day that I've been alive long enough to finally be a grandma."

The fussing between the twins settled and everyone exchanged a knowing, loving expression around the room. It might be messy, but messy was definitely worth it.

THE END

Summer at the Seaside

Find the series on Amazon: https://www.amazon.com/gp/product/B094TXN8S5

All books available for purchase on Amazon or through Kindle Unlimited.

Divine ApPOINTment by Ray Anselmo
https://www.amazon.com/dp/B093YQN Y9M

Sara Pike isn't doing as well as she thinks she is.

In her mid-forties, the assistant pastor of one of northern California's more innovative churches has the trust of her boss, her congregation, and her two grown sons. But she still bears the scars of betrayal from one she trusted: her now ex-husband, whom she caught with another woman. She's kept up with her ministry – so well that the senior pastor orders her to take a vacation to get the black cloud from over her head.

Sara knows he's not wrong. Which means it's time for her to hop in her truck, head for her favorite place in the whole world – the Point Reyes National Seashore – and hope against hope that she can finally get past the grief for her lost marriage. Even so, she might need a miracle … or **for God to use the Point for a divine ap-Point-ment.**

From the Summer at the Seaside series comes a unique and inspiring romantic novella unlike any other – Ray Anselmo's Divine Appointment. **Hop in and enjoy the journey!**

No Ordinary Summer Romance by Annee Jones

https://amzn.to/3uO2nbO

He's there on a whim. She's there to help her aunt. They're both missing something. Can it be each other?

"Find your Perfect Match this summer at the seaside..." The Forever Yours matchmaking agency is hosting a vacation package week in Seaview, Florida. Taking a break from her busy but unrewarding life in Chicago, Callie Winthrop has come to town to find respite at her beloved Aunt Fran's bed and breakfast. When the CEO of Forever Yours – who just happens to be staying at the inn for the event – offers Callie the opportunity to attend the activities and meet the most eligible bachelors in the country, how can she say no?

Jackson Thorne, a successful Tampa contractor, can't believe the nerve of his brother, who actually thought it was a good idea to sign him up for a matchmaking vacation this summer. Jackson acknowledges, however, that he has been avoiding commitment ever since his last relationship ended in tragedy. Hence it may actually be good for him to start dating again – much as he would hate to admit it. Maybe there's even a chance he could meet the woman of his dreams this summer?

Meet Me at Sunset by Theresa Oliver
smarturl.it/mmas

The flames of first love are volatile, consuming everything in its path, becoming the experience of a lifetime. The same was true with ours. He was my first love, my only love… and I was his.

I first met him in high school, and love hit me hard, slamming into me with its all-consuming flames engulfing my heart.

We were too young to fall in love, too young to experience anything so powerful… but we did.

We had dated through high school, and everyone said it wouldn't last. They were right.

On the night of our high school graduation, he asked me to meet him at sunset at our spot on the beach, on Sunset Beach, and we would get married. I didn't hesitate. But he never showed... and I never knew why.

Now, seven years later, he's back with an explanation, but I'm no longer the person I once was. The blaze that once burned bright and consumed my heart has died, having been extinguished long ago.

Now, can we fan the embers of our love into flames again, or will the forces that pulled us apart consume us both? Ours is a volatile first love consuming everything in its path. But will we survive it?

Meet Me at Sunset is a story of first love and loss, begging the question... what would you give to have a second chance with your first love?

Meet Me at Sunset is a sweet, clean contemporary mafia romance about first love and second chances. Check it out along with the rest of the titles in the Summer at the Seaside series!

Searching for Summer by Lorah Jaiyn
https://www.amazon.com/gp/product/B093YRPNFC

Summer Hughes married her sweetheart right out of high school. When she finds herself served with divorce papers after almost three decades, she retreats to Cape Manatee, a tiny town on the east coast of Florida. A favorite getaway as a child, Summer hides away to lick her wounds and try to figure out what went wrong.

Jerry Hughes throws himself into work to avoid his shattered heart caused by a divorce he doesn't want. When his company offers to send him to lead a project in Florida, he agrees in an instant. New state, new people, no memories.

As Summer falls in love with the quaint little town, a woman thrusts a two-year-old into her arms and vanishes. Jerry discovers that the development he's in charge of will destroy the entire area, and people are pushing to run him out of town.

When Summer and Jerry cross paths on the beach, will they take it as a sign that fate is telling them they're meant to be together? Or will outside influences from the town itself destroy any chance they have of reconciliation?

Summer at Spindrift Cottage by Kaitlynn Clarkson

http://mybook.to/summer-at-spindrift

He's hiding a secret that could ruin everything. She trusts him until it comes out. Will it be the end of love? Or can they learn to be honest with each other?

Ella Harwood has the perfect life. Chef in a trendy seafood restaurant in Seattle. Family and friends close by. Single and loving it (and no, she's not looking for love, thank you).

So it's a shock when she suddenly loses her job. Now how is she going to pay for her cute inner-city apartment?

Her mother comes up with the perfect solution: Ella can spend the summer caring for their grandmother's rambling B & B in Cockleshell Bay so Gran can take a vacation.

Cockleshell Bay? In the middle of nowhere? Ella has no intentions of doing any such thing.

But she soon finds herself out of options and on her way to Cockleshell Bay.

Things get off to a rocky start when the locals assume she's part of some conspiracy amongst the rich and famous to buy up all the houses in the area, but she's determined to stick it out, no matter what they think. It doesn't help that she has a secretive guest who goes off each day to do - what? No one knows, and the rumors abound.

When a storm comes, Ella finds herself forced to spend time with her reclusive but attractive neighbor, who also happens to be helpful around the house.

As they spend time together, Ella gets to know Flynn better, but what about the rumors? Is Flynn the person everyone thinks he is? Will Ella be able to trust him when it counts? Or is he hiding a secret that could ruin everything?

Also by Regina Walker

Sunshine and Starfish is my first contemporary romance novella. I recently released a sweet/clean historical romance—*A Maid for Mason.* I have 2 sweet/clean mail-order bride novels coming out around the holidays. Keep your eyes open for *A Christmas Comfort for Elsie* in November 2021 and *A Christmas Candle for Eleanor* in December 2021.

To get updates about my new releases, please join my mailing list here: http://eepurl.com/g4_zrf

A Maid for Mason
http://books2read.com/maidformason

Mary Ann grew up in New York, as the daughter of an immigrant Irishman and a housemaid. Her coming of age was marked as the day she started work. The young woman of the house where she is employed is full of wild ideas and tries to drag Mary Ann into her schemes. One such scheme finds Mary Ann agreeing to exchange letters with a man settling in the west, which gives her a reason to imagine wide-open skies and life on the frontier.

Widowed at a young age, Mason has been left to care for his son, James, and his land alone. They have enough to get by, but it's hard to work the land, run the cows, and keep a toddling boy out of trouble. His sister and her husband help where they can, and they keep offering to take his son for a time, but Mason can't bear the thought of letting the boy go live with them. Love is the last thing on his mind as he tries to figure out how to keep moving forward.

⚠ Hannah, Mason's sister, doesn't think her brother should be trying to do everything alone. He won't listen to her pleas to do something to find a wife, so she takes matters into her own hands. ⚠

♥ **Can two people, tricked by a sister with good intentions, find love on the frontier?** ♥

My first series is the *Then Comes Hope* collection. This is not a sweet/clean series. This is edgy, inspiring Christian fiction about really hard life circumstances, such as suicide, drug addiction, abuse, and teen pregnancy. These books don't shy away from things that are hard, but they all feature a hopeful thread and ending.

Edgy, bold fiction that navigates grief, suicide, substance abuse, domestic violence, and teen pregnancy. The *Then Comes Hope Collection* doesn't mince words as these families face difficult circumstances.

The series kicks off with *We Go On (http://books2read.com/wegoon)*, where you will meet Liz and Josh as they are barreling through the loss of their son and the consuming grief that follows. After Colby took his own life, his parents discovered some of his secrets, including the beautiful golden horse he called Dusty.

The next installment, *Still With Us* (*http://books2read.com/stillwithus),* continues to the introduction to Tammy and Ella as Ella spirals out of control. Addicted to drugs and clinging to an abusive boyfriend, her choices lead her to dark places. While Liz shows up for Tammy in many ways, Tyler drops everything to come to Ella's aid.

The third book, *We Grow Together* (*http://books2read.com/wegrowtogether),* introduces new characters, Riley Hamilton and Kyle Green. A bonfire, alcohol, and a night unsupervised, and Riley finds herself pregnant. At first, the odds are against her and it seems there is no hope for the baby growing in her womb. But Tyler and Ella (all grown up since we last saw them in *Still With Us)* show up and love on Riley, showing her that all hope is not lost.

Grab all three books to see how these families navigate the most painful things, and how good horses help them on their journey and bring them together.

About the Author

Regina Walker thinks a pen is her best friend and she loves taking a blank page and turning into a story to share. Whether her characters are facing tough life situations or looking for love, she hopes that their stories will inspire you and that you will close her books with a sense of something gained at the end.

Regina is an Oklahoma import, although she was born and raised in the beautiful state of Colorado. She likes to curl up on the couch and binge-watch crime shows with her hard-working husband. When she's not wrestling with a writing project, she can be found wrangling their children, riding their horses, or working around their small hobby farm.

Made in the USA
Columbia, SC
08 April 2022

58678070R00095